Richard Blaze and the King's Code

An Empire Revealed

I0417850

Ravi Pandya

ISBN: 0-983-44101-4
ISBN-13: 978-0-983-44101-4

DEDICATION

This book is for my sister Shefali.

Table of Contents

ACKNOWLEDGMENTS

I would like to thank my good friend Bailey for helping me and my parents for encouraging me to finish and editing after I was done. This book would not have been completed without them.

This page was intentionally left blank.

This page was intentionally left blank.

MY CAMPING TRIP MAKES SOME WEIRD NOISES

Rick

It was a night at Wolf Mountain a few years ago that I will never forget. The stars looked like millions of tiny lanterns in the beautiful, dim orange sky. The pond was so cold that when you got in, it felt like you jumped into a pile of ice cubes. It glistened as the bright moon towered and shimmered above all else. The only evidence of the barren trees around the pond were owls hooting from them as the harsh winter had shown no mercy on the lush green leaves once visible in better temperatures.

Hold up. Before I go any further with this, I guess I should introduce myself.

Chapter One

My name is Richard Blaze, but everyone calls me Rick. I'm going into eighth grade, and am on summer break. I live in Danville, Virginia, a small city near the southern border of North Carolina and Virginia. The mountain that I refer to as Wolf Mountain is actually near the community center, and doesn't have an actual name; everyone in the community just calls it that.

My birthday is October 15th. I have dark brown hair and always wear a watch, just to be able to keep track of time because I'm the kind of guy who likes to follow a schedule. I'm not exactly athletic, but can play sports fairly well. My life has been pretty normal, you know, the usual; playing video games, going to school, hanging out with friends, and other things...until the incident I'm about to describe to you.

But before I tell you that story, I've got to give you some advice. I don't know who you are, but if anything like what I am about to tell you happens in your life, do anything in your power to avoid the path I took. If you ignore my advice, don't blame me, because I have done everything I can to stop you.

Anyway, back to the story. A bunch of the local families had gotten together and decided to take all the neighborhood kids on our annual camping trip that weekend. We had to hike up the mountain so that we could set up our tents at the top. My mom had dropped me off to the mountain a bit late, so I had to take the hike by myself.

It was pretty late at night, maybe nine o'clock, so I couldn't see everything around me, but I'll tell you what I saw.

The slope was at about a forty degree angle, so it was pretty hard to hike up, especially since I had to carry my sleeping bag and clothes for the next day. There were a lot of small trees and shrubs growing in random places, none of which I could recognize. The ground had a clear trail up, probably the way to get to the top, so I followed it. There were also some giant gray rocks just lying there. Well, I didn't think they could have done anything anyways.

I was always afraid of the dark. The dark meant that I couldn't see every detail that made up whatever was going on around me, so if there was any kind of noise, I wouldn't know what made it. That's pretty much what was going through my head at that point.

A few minutes after I started up the mountain, I heard a sound. It was a low rustling sound coming from somewhere deep inside the bushes. I didn't think much of it at first, until I heard it again. That time, I got pretty scared because it was the *exact* same sound I had heard before. After that, I started to walk slower because I was being a lot more careful of where I was going. I didn't want anything to happen. Even the whistling of the wind sounded creepy. I got scared of just about anything after that.

When I finally got to the top, I saw a spectacular sight. In an instant, I figured out why they had chosen this place for a camping site. It was beautiful. There was a small pond in the middle that was sparkling in the moonlight. There were also a few bushes here and there. It was dark out, so it looked somewhat haunted because of the owls hooting from what seemed like nowhere. Aside from that, the place was great.

There were tents scattered in random places around the pond, and I saw some people were still having trouble setting one up. Every time they would put it upright, it looked perfect, until it collapsed again. I figured that it was just a defective tent, because it seemed like they were setting it up correctly.

I looked inside every tent in search of my friends, but instead of finding them, I would always get the same stare that said *who the heck are you?* I guess I wasn't exactly a well known person. Even in my own community. I looked for about ten or fifteen minutes, until I came to the only tent I hadn't looked in yet.

Just my luck. They have *to be in the last tent I look in, don't they?* I thought.

The tent was sitting on the edge of the pond, on the opposite side of the mountain we had hiked up. It was the farthest out and barely visible form the other side. I guess that's why I didn't see it at first. But I should have known, my friends have a tendency to go to extremes-they make sure they stand out. Or not get noticed.

I took a peek inside and found my four closest friends sitting and hanging out together in the tent: Alexandra, Roy, Xavier, and Lauren.

Chapter One

"What's wrong, Rick?" was the first thing that was said. I guess I still had a frustrated/scared look on my face.

"N-Nothing," I responded to Lauren. She had a thing for being able to tell what was going on in your mind. It was kind of creepy sometimes, or maybe she just knew people that well.

I guess I should tell you about my friends before I go any further. Roy had very dark brown, messy hair and almost always wore jeans. He had bangs that went down to his eyes, which were also brown, and he was usually a jokester, but could give a good death stare. Xavier had black hair and hazel eyes, and loved to play any kind of game he could get his hands on. He had perfectly straight hair that went halfway down his forehead. Alex was an athletic, dirty blonde kid with blue eyes. Her hair was wavy and was about down to her shoulders. She loved playing sports, especially soccer, like me. Lauren had straight, light brown hair past her shoulders, green eyes and pretty much *always* wore a sweater. And I already told you about that uncanny ability of hers.

"Then what took you so long?" said Lauren with curiosity and a hint of doubt on her face. She knew I was lying.

"Well…my mom dropped me off late," I said. I left out the part about getting scared and the weird noises I kept hearing.

After that, we stayed up talking for a few hours, and I was enjoying myself. I actually forgot about my hike up the mountain, until I heard it again, a low rustling sound coming from somewhere deep inside the bushes.

That time I got really scared. My breath got heavy, and I began to look around. I started for the door, but then I heard a loud horn. Everyone knew what that meant. Time for bed. No going outside and no talking whatsoever. At first, I wondered why we had to sleep so early, until I glanced at my watch. It read twelve-thirty.

Oh. I hadn't realized how much time had gone by.

I changed into my pajamas and climbed into my sleeping bag. *Finally,* I thought, *time to relax.* I tried really hard to fall asleep, but for some reason, I couldn't. I kept thinking about what had happened on the way up the mountain. I forced myself to think of other things, and eventually I fell asleep. Dreams found me. My dream was a bit odd that night. I dreamed that I was standing in front of a pack of wolves. I was on the edge of the pond on Wolf Mountain, or at least I think it was the same place. I believe they were trying to tell me something, but all I heard were random whispers of gibberish that made no sense at all.

I was suddenly awakened by the sound that I had grown to fear so much- a low rustling sound coming from somewhere deep inside the bushes. I was really starting to wonder what was making that noise, so I crept outside as slowly and quietly as I could. I had to, because if anyone found out I was up at that hour; I would be in huge trouble. So I decided to not wake anyone up.

As I opened the tent to go outside, a gust of cold wind came straight into my face. It was somewhat refreshing, but I quickly stepped outside and closed the tent with hopes that my friends wouldn't wake up and notice I was gone.

The first thing I realized when I went outside was that I was still wearing my pajamas. That didn't exactly matter, except that they were thin so I was freezing my butt off. The second thing I realized was that I couldn't see anything, which wasn't good because the whole reason I came outside in the first place was to see what was making the noise.

I figured I could sit down and wait for a few minutes so that my eyes would adjust. I waited…and waited…and nothing happened. I thought for a while that I was just going to have to wait until the break of dawn because I couldn't see anything and therefore could not go back into my tent. Until I saw something it wasn't much, but it was something. At least my eyes were adjusting. I finally made out that it was a bush, just the thing I needed. It seemed like it was a few feet away, not that difficult to get to.

I slowly got up and headed toward the bush. It was farther away than I thought it would be. It had looked small from where I was sitting, but I soon realized it was much bigger. I don't think it would even be specified as a bush anymore. I think it was about six to seven feet tall, a lot taller than I was. It was a really dark shade of green and looked like the branches inside were pretty far apart, so I could go inside it easily. I didn't care though, I was sleepy and it was a bush, that's all I needed to know.

I pushed aside a few branches so I could get a clearer view of what was inside. I instantly got scared. It wasn't the bush, but what was inside it. The animal I feared the most.

A dog.

I know, it sounds crazy, but yes, I was deadly afraid of dogs. You might be thinking, what happened to "a dog is a man's best friend?" Well, they were anything but my best friend. I had a horrible experience with dogs when I was little that I need not go into, and have been afraid of dogs ever since. The dog looked almost gray, and was no more than three feet tall, but it was enough to scare me.

I turned around and sprinted as fast as my legs would take me. I would do anything to get away from it and into my safe little tent. But as it turns out, thankfully, it didn't chase me. It almost seemed like it had been trained, because usually if you ran away from a dog, it would run after you. I ran all the way to the tent and suddenly stopped because I remembered something. My friends should *not* wake up.

My Camping Trip Makes Some Weird Noises

I slowly went inside and closed the tent behind me. I made sure my friends were still asleep, they all were. I got into my warm sleeping bag and tried to fall asleep again, but couldn't because I was in constant fear of the dog bursting in. I tried to get that out of my head by trying that counting sheep trick to fall asleep. I never got how that worked on other people, because it would get me thinking about math, and I would never be able to fall asleep thinking about math. Then I guess that counting sheep didn't help my problem of staying awake. The only reason I finally fell asleep was because I was exhausted from the huge sprint I just took.

I hoped that I would dream about something happy because I was still completely freaked out about what had happened. But dreams never came. I think that was a good thing, because nightmares never got a chance to scare me.

The first thing I heard when I woke up was an alarming horn. It was much louder than the one the previous night; I think that was because it was supposed to wake everybody up instead of getting us to settle down.

Chapter One

I was the first one up of all my friends, so I got ready and had the job of waking everyone up. We had made a pact the night before; whoever wakes up first will wake up everyone else.

If you've never woken up a twelve year-old kid, I'll warn you now: it's a lot more difficult than you would think. I spent the next half an hour waking everybody up. We had about one hour after the horn went off to get ready and be outside. So they were all rushing to change their clothes and get outside to wash their faces in the pond and get fresh.

After that was all sorted out, we went to the other side of the pond where everybody was supposed to gather after we were done getting ready.

"Everybody quiet!" shouted our chaperone over the voices of everyone talking. Suddenly the talking subsided.

A word about him, his name is Tim and he has a loud leader-like voice. He can be harsh, but most of the time pretty nice. He has short, dark brown hair and is about six feet tall. Other than that, I don't know anything about him.

"All right, so what you have to do is to…"

I was really tired, and my attention span was never very long anyways. I started thinking about random stuff, and had absolutely no idea what Tim was saying at that point. After about five minutes of me dozing off and him giving instructions, my brain decided to get back to reality.

"Everybody knows what they have to do now?" said Tim. Everybody nodded, except me.

We started walking to the bushes next to the pond, and I was still confused.

"So what exactly are we doing now?" I asked Roy, "I kind of wasn't paying attention."

"Well, basically we have thirty minutes to find something that looks interesting from the mountain and isn't yours then show it to Tim and after everybody has shown him, we'll start our hike down the mountain," he replied as we approached the bush.

"Why are we doing this?" I asked.

"He says it's a scavenger hunt."

I had an idea; we could look in the giant bush I had found the night before! I was about to tell my friends about how I knew about the bush, but instead lied and said that I needed to check on something in the tent. My plan was to go there, and then pretend to find the bush for the first time, and call them over there. It most certainly did not work out that way.

I went into the tent and pretended to check on something so that they wouldn't get suspicious of what I was doing. When I came out, I went to the place where I saw the huge bush that night. But what I saw was... nothing. It wasn't there. My first thought was that I was in the wrong place. But I was sure it was the exact same spot. My footprints from earlier were even there to prove it. That didn't compute, how could something or someone take down such a huge bush overnight without anyone noticing? And what was even more stunning was that there was absolutely nothing. I know, I said that already, but there was no sign that there had ever been a bush there in the first place. I mean, if it was cut down, there should at least be a stump or a hole in the ground. I didn't get how that was possible.

While I was walking, I put a stick in the ground everywhere my footprints were so I could come back later. I tried to pretend like nothing strange ever happened, but that would be hard with Lauren around, and I probably looked really confused. I did my best to stay away from her. I got back and didn't say a word.

"Was everything okay?" asked Alex.

"Was what okay?" I asked, confused.

"You went to check on something, right? Was everything okay?"

"Oh, that, right. Everything's fine," I lied.

"All right…" but she didn't sound so sure.

Alex let it go. I also decided that I shouldn't dwell on what had just happened so much, or I would get really stressed.

We finally got back to finding the things, though it didn't take as long as I expected. When we were done, I had found some kind of ancient arrowhead that had a short stick at the end, so I figured at one point it must have been part of a bow and arrow. Xavier had found an oddly curved stick that was really well polished and smooth for some reason. Alex had found a string that was very flexible, definitely man-made, and very old. Lauren had found a fossilized footprint that probably belonged to something in the dog family, which was really creepy, so I stayed away from it. Roy had found a long stick that oddly seemed like the back end of the arrowhead that I'd found.

When we showed it to Tim, he seemed really impressed and said he had never seen five kids find such interesting artifacts so quickly. He also pointed out that we were the first ones done, so we got a head start down the mountain if we wanted. I really wanted to get out of there because of all the weird things that had happened to me over the course of the last two days.

"Lets go, I really want to get down from here," I told my friends.

"Why? The view is really nice up here," said Xavier.

I hesitated for a second. I didn't know what to say, and they were all staring at me, waiting for an answer. "High elevations scare me," I lied.

"Okay, good enough," said Xavier, "let's go."

As we headed down the mountain, I was able to see it in more detail because it was about one in the afternoon, instead of about nine at night. There were still random bushes and rocks everywhere; and I now saw that most of them were wilted and dying.

You would think that hiking down a mountain would be much easier than climbing up, but that's not at all true. If anything; it's worse. That's because you're in constant fear of slipping on a weak part of land or gravel, so you have to be extra careful; especially if you don't have the right kind of shoes. And if you get really unlucky and do slip, you're in for a ride, and not a fun one at that.

Anyway, let's not get into the details of what would happen to your body when you slip down a forty degree angle mountain. So, when we were about a fourth of the way down, I heard voices behind us. I looked back to see a big group of people. Sometimes big groups going on a trip like this wear the same color shirts or have T-shirts printed for the group so every one is easily identified like all wearing red or green shirts.

Well, our trip down wasn't exactly exciting, except when I almost slipped and one of those giant gray rocks provided a place for my foot to land and just about saved my life. When we were nearing the bottom of the mountain, I was as relieved as I had ever been in my life.

Chapter One

But my relief didn't last long; that was because I heard it again; a low rustling sound coming from somewhere deep inside the bushes. I knew what was around, dogs. I hate dogs. I think I've mentioned that before, right?

That's when I did the only thing my brain could process at the moment; I ran like heck. It was probably the fastest I had ever run before; I left everyone behind me in dust. When I finally got to the bottom of the mountain, my only thought was:

Is my mom here yet?!

I really hoped so, but judging by my luck, she probably wasn't. I was wrong, and it was one of the only times in my life I had been happy to have been wrong about something (and I'm not wrong often). For some reason, she seemed to have known something was wrong, I could tell by the look on her face. She looked really concerned. When I got in the car, I told her to leave right away. She didn't hesitate, I'm happy to say. Thankfully, our house wasn't very far away, so I got home in about five minutes and when I got inside; I collapsed on the couch.

My Camping Trip Makes Some Weird Noises

Our house was kind of small, only one story with three bathrooms and four bedrooms. There was a living room, family room, and a kitchen. I live with my mom, dad and one older sister who is two years older than me. We don't have a bad relationship with each other like most siblings do; we take care of and help each other whenever possible. My mom and dad aren't that bad either, yeah sometimes they get mad at us if we do something wrong, but they say it's for our own good, so I deal with it.

About twenty minutes after I got home, I constantly received phone calls, always the same thing, "What happened? Why did you leave so suddenly?" I gave them all the same answer, I missed home. I think they bought it; for a while. But I couldn't trick Lauren; she could tell something was wrong just by the sound of my voice. I guess I should have known that Lauren wouldn't buy that many lies.

I finally decided to tell her the truth, but not all of it. I left out the part about the huge bush disappearing, and my crazy dream. I just told her how that weird rustling had been really creepy, and that's why I ran off so quickly. I think she believed me. At least that was off my shoulders.

The rest of the day was completely normal; at about three o'clock I went into my room and started playing video games for a few hours. The gray chair in my room is a big, soft and comfy bubble chair. I sit in it and either read or play video games whenever I want to use up some time. My room was pretty small; it only had space for my bed, a small black desk, and a television with a game system hooked up to it, and of course my bubble chair. I also had a closet where I kept all my clothes (which wasn't much) and put all my other random junk on the floor.

A while later, I had just a little bit of food when mom served dinner but it was enough to fill me up. I immediately went to bed because I was so worn out from that day. Dreams can be a lot of things; they can be nice, where everything is perfect, they can be just flat out weird where completely random things happen, they can be a nightmare, or they can be trying to tell you something.

My Camping Trip Makes Some Weird Noises

The brain works in mysterious ways, sometimes, if something is about to happen to you in real life, say getting whacked on the head with a stick, it'll happen in your dream and you'll wake up and subconsciously know what to do. It's happened to me before, and trust me it can be really helpful. That night, my dreams were definitely trying to tell me something, but in a different way. It was the same dream I had had the night before; I was standing in front of a pack of wolves, but this time; it was different. I could actually understand some of what they were trying to tell me.

Come to us. That's the only thing I understood. Has it ever happened to you that you wish you could control your dream to find something else out? That's pretty much exactly how I felt. It started to fade away, but I couldn't ask them where I had to go. When I woke up; I realized something. One of the wolves looked exactly the same as the dog I had seen in the bush. Then I realized something else, it wasn't a dog I had seen, it was a wolf.

Most of the morning, I was in shock. It was the wolves; they had been making all the rustling, probably trying to get my attention. Or it was all a huge coincidence that the same wolf I had seen in the bush was in my dream. Either way, I still didn't see how the wolves got into my dreams in the first place. Or I was just dreaming a regular dream. But dreams never happen the same way twice, do they?

I hoped they did because I wanted to forget everything ever happened and live a normal life; but I knew that *something* was going to happen, and soon. I thought everything was going to be normal, but that was the week that changed my life.

BACK TO THE MOUNTAIN

Rick

The day started out boring, so I invited my friends over. I had invited Alex, Roy, Xavier, and Lauren; as I usually did. It started out normal; we were talking, having fun, and just hanging out in my room. Until I heard it again; but you probably already know what I'm going to say though, a low rustling sound coming from somewhere deep inside the bushes.

"I-I'll be right back, okay?" I said.

"Is everything all right? Where are you going?" asked Xavier.

"Uh, yeah everything's just fine, I'll be outside,"

Chapter Two

"Okay, see you in a bit,"

I walked out of my room, and to the front door. I hesitated, I don't know why; I guess I sensed that something somewhere in the world had just gone wrong. I had no idea how right I was.

═══════════════════════════════════════

It was dark and there was a large silence in the courtroom. The walls were usually a brilliant shade of white in sunlight, but something seemed to be wrong; the walls had turned a depressing shade of black. That had only happened once, and that was the last time the kingdom was under attack. The silence was suddenly broken by the sound of the palace doors opening and someone running in.

"Sir, sir, we have a problem," said the stranger while still gasping for air.

"What is it?" boomed the deep voice of the king.

"Th-the invasion is starting, their numbers are far more then we expected, and they have come earlier than we thought, sir, we have about one hour at max."

"Gather everyone and tell them that if they can fight, they shall."

Back to the Mountain

"That's the problem sir, everybody is already there, and ready to fight, but they still outnumber us."

"Then I will go myself and fight for my kingdom until my very last breath," was the king's brave response.

The king had always been fair and always fought for the welfare of his subjects. They were loyal subjects, and never disobeyed his command. The subjects loved their king, as he had always been the greatest king the land had ever known. He was brave, and fierce in battle, he was also honest, trustworthy, and truthful. It was for these very reasons that he was crowned king, though he had not a drop of royal blood in him.

The king went outside his palace with his guards to take one last look at how beautiful his kingdom was, and imagined what it might become if the invaders won the war. There were giant old trees everywhere and the ground was covered with fresh green grass. There were boulders scattered in the woods, and burrows of small animals. Some boulders were covering burrows; giving them protection and keeping in the warmth that was produced by the animal's bodies.

Chapter Two

The king thought about all of his finest moments; the day the crown was placed upon his head, the day after they won the last war, and so many others they were almost impossible to count. This kingdom had so many great triumphs and almost no failures. The empire had been the greatest of all, and that day was to decide whether it would perish or prevail once more like it had done so many times before.

The king took his guards to the battlefield and saw all of his subjects in formation; preparing for the battle. He saw all of his loyal subjects wearing their pure black armor; it was made of the strongest metal that was around. The king's armor was made of the same material, but was thicker and provided extra protection.

As he made his way onto the battlefield, everyone turned, faced him, and showed their respect by bowing their heads down as he made his way to the front row.

"My dear subjects, you have served me well. It does not matter if we win this battle or not; but just remember that our great empire will never die, if you keep the same thoughts and attitude you have these many years…" the great king was about to go on, until his voice was drowned out by the battle cry of the invaders.

As I walked out the door, a gust of wind blew against my face; and the world suddenly seemed quieter, not peaceful; but depressed, like something horrible had just happened. Yet nothing seemed wrong, well not to me anyways. When I got outside to my front porch, I started looking for any bush nearby. Our porch was made of gravel, and had grass growing on either sides of it. The garage was the only other part of the house you could see from the front; besides the door. As you went around to the left side of the house; there was a side yard. It was mainly grass, but had a couple bushes; so I decided to check there.

As it turned out, there was something there. I saw a dark figure inside the bush of what looked to be a dog. I knew that wasn't true, because I figured out that the wolves were the ones behind the mysterious rustling. I approached it slowly and cautiously, making sure that it didn't flee. When I finally got to the bush, I parted the branches to see a wolf. It was a light shade of gray, and had a few black streaks of fur going down its back. It looked very familiar, but I just couldn't figure it out.

Then it hit me; it was the same wolf I had seen in my dream and in the disappearing bush that night at Wolf Mountain. *Did this wolf follow me to my house?* The idea that a wolf had been stalking me was sort of creepy. I hoped that that wasn't the case. For a while we just kept staring at each other because I was in a state of confusion, shock, and doubt. It was kind of awkward. The only other thing I could think of doing was to run. So I ran.

I sprinted back to my house, kicked the door open, and kept running, but then stopped about one foot short of the hallway that lead to my room. I decided that I should walk back in casually as if nothing strange had happened outside. As I walked in, the room suddenly got quiet and everybody was staring at me.

"I have to go home, sorry," said Alex.

"Uh…yeah, so do I," said Roy.

After everyone was done saying they had to go, I wondered why that had happened.

"Why do you have to leave so suddenly?" I asked.

Back to the Mountain

I got no response, just as I had expected. They probably thought I had been acting weird, and decided to go home while I was outside. After they all left, I got really bored again, so I took a short cat nap.

About an hour later, I awoke to the sound of soft footsteps slowly coming into my room. Usually my parents wouldn't walk so slowly when they were about to wake me up, so I wondered what was up. I opened my eyes to see who it was. As it turned out, it wasn't anybody in my family at all. My vision was somewhat blurred because I had just woken up and my eyes weren't open all the way. The figure seemed no more than three feet tall, and seemed to be wearing a gray sweatshirt. I wondered who I knew that could be that tall (or short). They were still walking in very slowly, which gave my eyes time to adjust. When they did; I soon realized that it wasn't a human at all. It was the wolf again.

"Go away! Shoo! What are you doing here? How did you get inside my house?!" I screamed.

All I got was a blank, stern stare; as if it was trying to tell me something. Once I calmed down, the wolf's expression changed; it looked worried, concerned; like it needed my help desperately. I got up and approached the wolf and reached my hand out to see if it would react. It did nothing; just stood there.

"What is it, is something wrong?" I asked it, thinking that I sounded pretty stupid since I was asking a wolf a question.

It shook its head up and down. Did it understand me? I didn't think that was possible. I suddenly realized how it got in; I had left the door open. I led it back to the front door, stepped outside, and motioned for it to leave the house. Its head drooped and it looked almost sad. It reluctantly stepped outside and glanced at me one last time before it walked away. I wondered where it was going to go.

The king was about to charge and attack the invaders, just when someone ran up to him and was about to start speaking. The king recognized him, he had been sent on a mission. If he had succeeded; the kingdom would be safe. If not, they would have to do their best to defend themselves.

"Where are they?" boomed the voice of the almighty king.

"I could not get even one of them to come with me; I am very, very sorry sir. I have failed."

"You have not only failed, but you have put the entire kingdom in jeopardy, at the mercy of the invaders!"

"I…I am aware of that sir."

"Since you could not get them to come; you shall have to fight alongside me and all the others," the king said.

"Very well, I shall do as you say."

As the door was about to close, a gust of wind came again. But after it was gone, it was a similar feeling to the last time that had happened; it seemed like something went wrong again. Only this time; it felt like I was the one who had done something wrong.

When I closed the door, I went back into my room and laid down on my bed to think about the past few days and how all of the weird things that had happened to me were somehow connected.

Chapter Two

The first thing was the rustling sound, I thought, *which I later found out was the wolf. The next thing was the dream when the wolves were talking gibberish. After that, it was the disappearing bush, and I found a wolf inside so they have to be related in some way. The next incident was the dream where the wolves had said* come to us. *The final weird thing was the wolf following me to my house and inside as well. What was even more odd was that that wolf had been both in my dream and in the bush so I guess that that particular wolf must be part of the reason all of this is happening to me.*

After I was done thinking, I had dinner and later went to sleep. My dream was the same one I had been having for the last couple of days. This time, I was able to understand a lot more of what they were saying.

Come to us. Back to Wolf Mountain, the help of you and your four friends is urgently needed. This is the only way we are able to contact you without you running away; as you have done before. We wish that you could have been here earlier, but if you come now; you shall be just as great a help as you would have been before.

Back to the Mountain

Remember this, pass the message onto your friends; and come quickly. We need you.

I suddenly sat bolt upright in my bed freaked out about what had just happened.

It was just a dream, it doesn't mean anything. I kept telling myself, but deep down, I knew that wasn't true.

I got up out of bed because if I wake up after sleeping, I can't go back to sleep again- I'm weird that way. Anyways, after I got up, I went into the kitchen to get some cereal. While I was eating, I debated whether or not I should do what the wolves in my dream said to do. I decided that it was more likely that I was dreaming, because scientifically, I didn't think it was possible for someone to send messages though dreams.

Man. At that time, I didn't know how wrong I was.

Later, I called my friends over again. They all came within half an hour and I decided to tell them the truth. All of it. I wanted to see what they would make of it all. It took maybe fifteen minutes to completely tell them what happened.

"What do you think?" I asked.

Chapter Two

"Well, I don't know what to think of the disappearing bush, but based on the facts, I'd say that the wolves desperately need our help. It seems like all of these incidents that occurred are connected to one thing; and I believe that it's the wolves." replied Lauren.

"But how do we know that it's all true then?" was Alex's logical question.

"We don't, but if we never check, how will we know? And what's the worst that could happen?"

"If it all turns out to be real and we might have just put our lives in danger," replied Alex.

"Come on, don't you want a little adventure in your life? We've all lived completely normal and somewhat boring lives, and up until now, we've never had a chance to make it exciting, haven't you ever wanted something big to happen to you?" Lauren said.

"Yeah, I guess I have always thought my life could be more exciting," said Roy.

"How about the rest of you? Are you up for it?" asked Lauren.

"Yeah, I'm in," said Xavier.

"Same," replied Alex.

I hesitated, but I guess since I was the one who told them about it and all of the weird stuff had happened to me, I did not have much of a choice and also felt obligated to go.

All right, I'll go," I said.

After that, I packed some stuff, like food, water, a first aid kit, and a tent; in case we needed to camp out. I hoped we didn't because I really wanted to come back home sometime soon.

We decided to leave right away, and make sure our parents didn't notice that we were gone. The first thing that came to my mind was: *how will we get there if none of us can drive?* My question was answered as soon as we went out the door and started walking. It was a dreadful walk because we were carrying all the supplies.

As we walked down the street, we were all silent for some odd reason. Maybe they were debating whether or not this whole thing would turn out to be real. I didn't want to think about it too much, or I would get all stressed out, and that doesn't help anyone. So I decided to look around at the scenery to keep my mind off everything that had happened in the past few days.

Chapter Two

My street was silent, and there were houses with trees planted on small patches of grass between every one. I guess that was the builders' way of showing that they cared about nature. I didn't think that was helping them because they were the people who tore down the land in the first place.

The road there had a lot of twist and turns, but since we weren't in a car, that didn't matter. Our walk took about forty-five minutes. We were probably a lot slower than we could have been considering we had a heavy bag of supplies and a separate bag with the tent in it.

When we got to the mountain, I was as tired as ever. I think everyone else was too, and I didn't have the energy to hike up that mountain again.

"Why don't we take a break?" I asked them.

"Sure," replied Xavier.

"Sounds good," Roy said.

So we took a break. We just sat on the ground and ate. We all had a sandwich and a glass of water. I had packed ten sandwiches in all; two for each of us. There were also about three gallons of water (which added a *lot* of weight to our bags) and some apples; you know, to keep us healthy. I never got the phrase "an apple a day keeps the doctor away," because I love apples, usually eat them every day, and I've missed school for almost one full month before from being sick. Those apples certainly did *not* keep my doctor away.

It was about ten minutes later that we had all finished eating, but we decided to rest for a little while before making the steep hike up Wolf Mountain. After we were all rested up, it was about four thirty. It just happened to be the hottest time of day, and we were hiking up a big mountain.

Great, just great. I thought to myself.

That one sandwich was barely enough to get me to the peak of the 1500 ft mountain. It was around a mile uphill and I would have died if it was any taller.

The first thing we decided to do was to go over to the pond and splash ourselves with cold water to cool off. That helped a lot, but it was also that it was cooling down outside anyways. The next thing I thought of doing was to go check if the bush was there, you know, the huge six or seven feet tall one.

Chapter Two

As I made my way to the other side of the pond, my friends followed me. When I got there, I forgot where the bush was, but luckily I found my old footprints from when I was running back to the tent that were somehow still there, but the easiest things to spot were the sticks in the ground. I thought that they would have been gone by then, but I guess not very many people had come that way nor had it rained since we left so we got lucky.

I started retracing my steps (literally) and found the same thing I had found last time that I had tried to find the bush; nothing.

"Shouldn't that huge bush you told us about be here?" inquired Roy.

"Well, this happened last time I checked too. I guess there's nothing here, my dream probably meant nothing. Let's go back."

Instead of going back, we all started arguing about if it was real or not. Many theories came up; it was all unreal, it was real but we were doing something wrong, we came too late so the wolves didn't need our help anymore, and a lot of others. We argued for a long time, long enough that now we didn't have much of a choice but to spend the night there because it got too dark and late in the day to head home.

"Um, I think we'll have to camp out here. It's getting dark and really late," I said. I didn't get any resistance from that decision. I think everyone wanted to stay and solve this mystery.

"Well, I want to go back, but I think you're right," replied Alex.

So it was settled; we were going to camp out there for the night, hopefully the last night. We took maybe ten minutes to set up our tent: and another ten to set up our sleeping bags. I had thought that we wouldn't be camping out, but we brought all the stuff just in case, still; I hadn't brought my pajamas. I then had to sleep in dirty, sweaty, and somewhat rough clothes; I'll tell you now; that was *not* a fun experience.

Even though it had been really hot that day, the night was still pretty cold. Luckily, my sleeping bag was thick, so I stayed warm and cozy all night. Unluckily, my dream was similar to the last few nights. Yup, you guessed it; the wolf dream.

Chapter Two

I was still standing in front of a pack of wolves, and I looked over to the side of the group and saw the same wolf that had followed me not only to my house, but into my room. As I looked around, I saw that there were fewer wolves then there had been last time I had that dream. I wondered why that was.

Thank you for answering our desperate call. You have come, but you only find us when darkness has complete control over light. It is the only time we can show ourselves without using much energy and we are less likely to get in harms way. Find us, and soon. You have done the right thing.

It seemed like my dream lasted for hours. I think that was because it was the only dream I had that night, and I couldn't wake up. When I finally woke up; it was maybe seven o'clock in the morning because the sun was so bright.. I couldn't stop thinking about the dream I had.

When darkness has complete control over light.

What could that have meant? I tried not to dwell much on it, but I couldn't stop thinking about it. I had to wake everyone else up; again. I was always a light sleeper, but my friends? Not so much. I hated having to wake them up. It got really annoying and frustrating at times. The easiest person to wake up was always Lauren. She was never much of a complainer either; which made it easier. Not easy, but easi*er*. Everyone else complained though; Alex, Roy, and Xavier.

Just like last time, after half an hour of trying to wake them up; Lauren and I had finally succeeded.

"Ugh, why do you always wake us up so early?" complained Roy.

"It's *seven thirty*," I said, "you got enough time to sleep. I had another dream last night, and I'll tell you guys while we eat breakfast."

"Okay, fine."

I hadn't thought that we would be staying there for long, so I had only packed two sandwiches for each of us. How silly of me. We ended up having to eat our other sandwiches for breakfast and drinking pond water because we had decided to save what water we had left; and since we were next to a pond we didn't want to waste any of our own water. The pond's water wasn't as dirty as we had expected; it actually tasted pretty clean seeing that nobody was out purifying it every day.

Chapter Two

"So, are you going to tell us about your dream?" asked Xavier.

"What? Oh, right that. Okay, so the wolves said that we were doing the right thing; but we could only find them when darkness has complete control over the light." I said, still confused about what that meant.

"So, what time would that be?" asked Xavier.

"That's what I was hoping you guys could help figure out." I said.

"Well, I have no idea what that could possibly mean, so I can't help you."

"We'll have to figure it out fast, because we have no food left, and then we would have to go all the way back to Rick's house to get more food just to come back here again," Lauren said.

"I agree with Lauren," I said, "so, since light and dark aren't physical things; I'm guessing it would have something to do with the time of day. And since they said that darkness controls the light; it would probably be late at night or really early in the morning."

I paused; thinking about what I had just said. It had actually made a lot of sense; the only time we could find the wolves was when we would usually be asleep.

"Hey Rick," said Lauren.

"What?"

"You said that you had seen a wolf in the bush before, right?"

"Yeah, what about that?"

"Well, what time do you think you saw it?"

"Maybe around two-"

I suddenly stopped; realizing something. Why hadn't I thought of it before? It was a simple, yet brilliant idea.

"Then maybe-"

"Maybe we can only find the wolves then." I said, finishing Lauren's sentence for her, "and that might be the darkest time of day; *when darkness has complete control over light*, remember? It has to be this, it just has to."

"I agree with Rick," said Alex.

"I guess it's settled, we're going to stay up pretty late tonight," I said.

Chapter Two

"It's great that we figured it out, but how can we survive another twelve hours or more on *no* food; just water?" Lauren pointed out.

"We'll just have to find some food," I said in a very leader-like voice.

We immediately went out to find some food because we were all on a full stomach and had the most energy that we would have all day. We all went separate ways so we would have better chances to find more food. We all left to go into the woods, and headed off.

I saw many bushes, but none with berries or any other fruit on them. I kept walking forwards, until I hit the edge of the peak. If I had taken one step forward; I would have slipped and fell to the bottom. That wouldn't have been fun. But luckily, I didn't slip. Instead, I started walking around the edge of the peak to see if I could find some berry bushes around there, but I never did.

I started walking back to our tent to see if anyone else had collected anything. As I was walking back, I heard voices, it seemed like they were arguing over something. I guess they were already at our tent. I walked toward the sound of their voices, because I was completely lost and had nothing else to follow. It took maybe ten minutes to get to them; I hadn't realized how far I had gone.

But when I finally found them, it wasn't even them at all! As I made my way to the clearing in the woods, I found my self face to face with two deer in the middle of a standoff. They were both facing each other and in a stance as if they were about to start ramming into each other. Their antlers were pretty big and were locked together.

I stood there, confused at why the sounds of their voices had led me there. I backed away slowly; making sure the deer wouldn't get startled and attack me. As soon as I got out of the clearing, I started sprinting back to where I thought our campsite was. Thankfully, I recognized my surroundings and made my way back.

When I got to the tent, I saw Lauren, Roy, Xavier, and Alex discussing something. I walked towards them and started thinking about the arguing voices I had heard.

They're definitely talking, but it doesn't seem like they are arguing, so I don't think they were the voices I heard. But then again, what else in this place could possibly talk?

Chapter Two

That left me thinking for quite a while, but I didn't dwell on it much.

"Hey, were you arguing about anything a few minutes ago, before I was here?" I asked.

"Not that I can recall, why?" answered Lauren.

"Because I heard some people arguing while I was heading back, and I figured it had to be you guys, unless something else that can talk is here, but I doubt it,"

"Or you're just going insane," suggested Roy.

"Shut up," I said.

"Oh, hey, I found a huge berry bush somewhere and I brought a ton back, want some?" asked Alex from about twenty feet away.

"Sure. Are they any good?"

"Yeah, they taste just like raspberries."

I walked over to where Alex was standing and tried one, he was right, they did taste like raspberries. They were small, round and light blue. It was somewhat peculiar because I had never seen a light blue fruit before.

"These could be called light blueberries, or actual blue raspberries," said Roy.

Back to the Mountain

"Blue raspberry flavoring comes from an actual fruit, genius," Xavier pointed out while eating some berries.

"Oh."

I glanced at my watch, wondering how much time had to pass before we could finally see that huge bush again, only if our theory was right. It was two-thirty, so we had about twelve hours to kill.

"We have about twelve hours before it becomes really dark and we go find the bush. What can we do? Any suggestions?"

"We can sit around and talk," said Alex.

"We could, but would we really have enough to talk about to keep us occupied for *twelve hours*?" asked Lauren.

"We can sleep for a while because we're going to be up really late, so we'll have to catch up on our sleep sometime. Why not now, while we're really bored?" suggested Lauren.

"Yeah, that's a pretty good idea, but let's sleep in a few hours," I said.

"Let's use both ideas," said Xavier, "we can talk for say, an hour, and then sleep for a while."

Chapter Two

"That works for me," replied Roy.

After a while, we got in our sleeping bags, and fell asleep.

WE GET TESTED

Rick

I was suddenly awakened by the sound of footsteps inside the tent. It turned out that both Lauren and Alex were already awake. It was dark out, which meant I had slept for quite a while. I checked my watch; it was about one-thirty, the perfect time to wake up since we were supposed to be at the bush - around two o'clock.

"Hey," I whispered, still pretty sleepy.

"Hey, let's wake up Roy and Xavier," said Alex.

"All right," I replied.

When we were all awake, we headed out of the tent. It was exactly the same as it had been the last time; pitch dark outside and extremely cold. I wondered how we would find the bush. That was when I saw a really bright light being shone on the ground in the shape of a circle.

"Hey, what's that?" I asked.

"I brought an emergency flashlight," responded Xavier.

"Ah, good thinking."

"Hold on, I'll give it to you so you can lead us to the bush."

"All right."

Xavier handed me the flashlight and then I shined it on the ground in the general direction I had seen the bush before. I was mostly looking for my old footprints. It took about two minutes to find them, so then we started following them.

When we got to the end of my footprints, there was nothing else there, just like last time I had tried to find it.

"This doesn't make any sense, it should be here," I said, sounding really frustrated.

"Wait," Lauren said, "check the time."

I looked at my watch and hit the "light" button so I could see what time it was, and then told everyone else.

We Get Tested

"It's about ten till two," I announced.

"Then I think it makes sense, the bush probably won't show up until two because it isn't the darkest time of day yet," said Lauren.

"Or maybe Rick was just hallucinating," joked Roy.

We waited for ten minutes, in hopes that the bush would show up like Lauren had predicted. As soon as my watch showed two o'clock, the air in front of us started shimmering, and we all suddenly fell to the ground.

"What's happening?" Roy muttered to himself.

Suddenly, a brilliant light shined from out of nowhere, in the place that the air had shimmered before.

"Look away," Lauren shouted, "it's too bright!"

We all averted our eyes, but could still see the light with our peripheral vision. As soon as the light died down, we looked back to where the light had come from. In its place was a huge, six or seven foot tall bush, giving out a dim light from the inside so we could see without the flashlight.

"It's like, glowing," Xavier pointed out.

That cleared up how I was able to see the bush before, even without a flashlight with me. I then did what I had done before; I went up to the bush and parted the branches to see what was inside.

"Hey Rick, isn't that the wolf you had told us about?" asked Xavier.

"Yeah, it is," I said

"You, um, called us here?" I nervously asked the wolf.

"Yes I did." it said.

"Whoa, did anyone else hear that?" I asked.

"Yeah, that was weird," said Lauren.

"Wow, maybe we're all hallucinating," said Roy.

"But how could we all be hearing the same things?" Xavier asked.

"Right, good point."

"I can talk, ask me a question." it said.

"Okay, so why did you call us here?" I asked.

"I will explain everything when you come back with me. Hurry, there is not much time." replied the wolf.

The wolf turned around, walked forward, and disappeared in to the bush.

"He said to follow him, so I think we have to go in the bush," I said.

We Get Tested

We each took turns walking cautiously into the bush where the wolf had disappeared. I went first, and I felt like I was in a new world. It was daytime and there were giant old trees everywhere and the ground was covered with fresh green grass. There were boulders scattered in the woods, and burrows of small animals.

"The reason you feel like you are in a new world is because you are," the wolf said.

I turned around to see Roy, Alex, Xavier, and Lauren behind me.

"Wait, what do you mean we're in a new world?" I asked.

"As I said, I shall explain everything to you. This is our world; the world of animals, called Neosolgis. This world is in parallel with yours. That bush you went through is one of the few connections between our two worlds. There are no humans here that I know of, except for you five.

"Long ago, some animals found this bush and left for the other world. All animals can interact with each other, so back then, the humans learned the tongue of the animals and our language was passed down for generations until someone, somehow thought that all humans were superior to animals, so they forgot our language, and since not all   animals knew of the portal back to this world, so they were forced into hiding and did not associate with humans.

"You five are very special, you are the only remaining humans that know our tongue and we need you desperately."

"Yes, you've told us that," I said, "but why?"

"I am getting to that. You have powers you do not know of yet and you are the only ones who can save us. We were at war, and the invaders captured our king. You five are the only ones that are capable of rescuing him."

"Wait-wait-wait, why can't anyone else do this?" asked Alex, "I mean, we're only kids!"

"You have powers that you know not of yet," said the wolf.

"Yeah, like what?" asked Alex.

"You must discover that on your own."

"I just noticed, you haven't told us your name," said Lauren.

"My name is Kevdak Silentall."

We Get Tested

"So, what do we do now?" I asked.

"Follow me," said Kevdak.

We followed Kevdak for a long time; we passed by a huge forest, but most of the plants looked almost dead. It was odd, the closer we got to where he was taking us, the deader the plants looked. We finally got to a huge hall that looked black and very depressing. There were wolves standing guard and many wolves inside as well. As many as there were, not one looked happy, they looked sad.

"Why is everyone so sad?" I asked.

"Our king was captured and this hall turns different colors depending on whether something good or bad happened. How the hall feels will reflect how everyone inside of it will feel. If you even try to smile, it will be next to impossible, try it."

I tried to smile, but my muscles failed to respond. I saw Lauren, Roy, Alex and Xavier try it and have the same result. Kevdak was right, it was next to impossible.

"But," said Lauren, "why did you bring us here?"

Chapter Three

"Because I need to show you what our kingdom has become since our king was captured, so that you do not back out of your mission."

"So why shouldn't we back out?" I asked.

"Because if you do, our state will eventually get worse, the kingdom will perish, and the foxes will take over the land."

"Wait, why the foxes?" asked Xavier.

"They were the ones who took King Olkin, I told you, did I not?"

"No, you did not," replied Alex.

"Yes, but please accept your mission."

We debated whether or not we would go and rescue their king, and finally came to the decision that we would go rescue The king.

"All right, we accept," I said.

"Good, but before you leave, you must be trained. It will be of much help if you five know how to fight."

"Why?" Alex inquired.

"Because you never know who you will bump into on your way there."

We Get Tested

"All right, when do we start our training?" I asked while anticipating how we would get trained.

"You will start tomorrow, two hours before dawn."

"Why so early?" complained Roy.

"If you would rather work in the scorching heat of the sun, by all means, it is fine by me."

"No, no! It's fine!"

For the rest of the day, Kevdak showed us around the kingdom and told us stories about the king and his greatness, including how he became the king in the first place.

"It was no more than twenty years ago, but I remember the story much better than most," started Kevdak while motioning for us to sit down, "anyway, the king was about fifteen years old, but very strong, courageous and caring considering his age. It was a bright summer afternoon and the woods seemed very peaceful. Young Olkin was out wandering when he heard a loud roar coming from very far into the woods. He then heard the scream of a wolf being attacked. He started running toward the sound and found a huge bear, about six to seven feet tall with dark brown fur. It was Belkas, the bear that all young wolves got told stories about. He would attack innocent animals just for fun. Belkas was the worst monster we had ever seen. Olkin went up to the bear and slashed it across the paw to free the wolf getting attacked. That wolf was me. I had gone out in search of Belkas because I thought I had the skill to best him with my own paws, but I was very wrong. Olkin had caught the bear by surprise, so that gave me the chance to escape. I remember the kings words exactly, 'Go back, this is too dangerous for one as young as you. I shall handle this beast.' So I ran back to my house as he stayed back and fought. He jumped at Belkas with all his might and knocked him onto the ground so he would have a greater advantage. Olkin slashed his paw across the bear's neck and caused it a great deal of pain. There was a huge puddle of blood not surprising given the size of the animal and soon after, the terrible Belkas died. Olkin returned to our village and told us about his feat. Belkas had caused our community a lot of pain and suffering for many years. Since the demise of the old queen we had been left without a ruler as she did not have any heirs. We were in dire need of a strong ruler and at the time no one else was as good as Olkin."

"Wow," said Lauren, "Olkin must have been a great wolf and king, no wonder you want us to rescue him."

"Yes, we are in desperate need of him right now."

It was very dark outside by the time Kevdak had finished telling us all of his stories, so he took us back to the castle and showed us to a room on the left side. It was somewhat big; it had five beds and a small, round table in the center. We all chose a bed and went straight to sleep. That was the first night in a while that I didn't dream about the wolves, I guess that was because they had nothing more to tell me , since we were already there.

I suddenly awoke to the sound of Kevdak's voice, "Get up! It is two hours before dawn! You must eat, and then get to your training!"

I had much trouble waking up because I had never gotten such little sleep before. One by one, we all slowly woke up, I was first, Lauren was second, Alex was third, Roy was fourth, and Xavier was the last.

We walked over to the table in the center of the room and saw that there was food waiting to be eaten by someone. I guess that someone was us. There were all kinds of vegetables that looked like they were cooked over fire, but there was nothing else on the table. I guess the wolves were vegetarian, but so was I, so it didn't really matter.

I picked up something that looked like corn and started eating it, turned out it was corn but just a different color. I have to tell you, it was really good, probably the best corn I had ever tasted; if it really was corn. You should try it sometime. Oh wait, I highly doubt that you would be able to go through a bush-portal and then start hanging out with talking wolves and...well, you get the point.

"Hey," I said with my mouth half full, "you *have* to try this corn-like thing! It's awesome!"

"We *have* to?" asked Roy while looking at a fried carrot with disgust.

"What I meant is that you *should* try it."

"I think I will, because I don't really like the idea of roasted vegetables."

Xavier rolled his eyes and said, "Corn *is* a vegetable, genius."

We Get Tested

"Either way, I bet it is way better than the others."

Roy picked one up and started eating it when a smile appeared on his face, "You were right, this is really good!"

When we had all finally finished eating about forty minutes later, a wolf I didn't recognize walked inside.

"Come with me," it said in a stern, female voice, "I will show you to your training grounds."

"Who are you?" I asked.

"I will tell you when we get there."

We walked outside the castle and got to a piece of completely flat land with training equipment lying on the ground.

"Okay, I'm pretty sure we're here, so who are you?" I asked.

"I am your teacher. Your master, whatever you would like to consider me as, but when you are talking to me, you shall call me Corvyre."

"We shall start by seeing how strong you are right now, so I know how much to train you before you are completely ready."

Chapter Three

Corvyre told us to lift some stuff that didn't look very heavy at first, but would make anyone's arms sore after a certain time. They were small, two feet long bars that were about three inches thick. It looked like it was made of metal, but whatever it was, it was very dense. I could barely carry it for more than forty-five seconds, and everyone else was pretty close. I was surprised to find that I actually held it up the longest.

"Very good Rick," said Corvyre.

"You must all now run around the edge of our training ground for as long as you can. When you feel like you need rest, you can stop, but that will be the end of your run."

After we all got into our places, she yelled, "Go!"

We all started out in a small sprint, but later slowed down because it was using too much energy. I had never been good at running long distances, just sprinting short distances. After about five minutes into it, I went into a slow jog so I would be able to go for a longer time. That worked for a while, but when about twenty-five minutes were up, I started to feel dizzy and my chest started hurting, so I was forced to stop.

We Get Tested

Unfortunately, I was the first one to stop. Roy stopped soon after, and I expected he was feeling the same as I was. Xavier and Lauren stopped at about thirty minutes, and their faces were bright red. Alex kept going for about five minutes more and then collapsed on the other side of the training grounds. We all ran towards her as fast as we could (which wasn't very fast since we had all just ran) carrying food and water. Corvyre sprinted faster than I could have ever run in my whole life, but I guess that's because she wasn't a human.

When we got over to where Alex was, Roy splashed some water on her face. She looked unconscious, so we let her sleep for a while because the training had to be done with all five of us. We all carried Alex back to the castle and put her in her bed. After a few hours, she woke up. We didn't go back to the training because the sun was up and it was starting to get too hot.

"How long was I out?" she asked, sounding very sleepy.

"It was about three hours. You should eat something," I said while helping her sit up.

Chapter Three

Corvyre then stormed into the room and started shouting, "What were you thinking?! You should have stopped running when you got tired! Not when you faint!"

"You said to run as long as I can, and that's exactly what I did," was Alex's smart answer.

"All right, good enough, but do not do that again. Because of you, we are one day behind schedule! You all must wake up even earlier tomorrow if we hope to catch up."

"Aw!" groaned Roy.

"Hey," Alex said weakly, "I have to eat something, I need energy."

I took some of the amazing corn out of the bag and gave it to her. She had a faint smile, "You were right before, it is awesome."

The rest of the day went by somewhat fast, but pretty much all we did was sit in our room and talk because it was warm outside and Alex still couldn't do anything. I wished it had been air conditioned, but I guess animals had not found a way to make that yet.

We Get Tested

Nothing else that happened that day was exciting. So I'll skip to the part where we go to sleep and have dreams. That night, I had a very peculiar dream. I saw myself standing on top of a mountain and there was air swirling around me. I mean, there's always air around me, but this was different, I could see the wind around me, it was a dark shade of white. After a while of staring at myself, the image changed and I was suddenly looking at Alex in the face. She was standing inside a volcano on a small rock. There was lava erupting behind her, but for some reason, it erupted everywhere except where she was standing. The lava was a bright red, the color of fire. There were smaller chunks of rocks disintegrating in it, so it looked *really* awesome. Next, I saw Xavier standing on a huge lily pad in the middle of a lake. The last word that would come to my mind was peaceful. There were huge waves coming from the right side, but going straight under Xavier; leaving him and his lily pad still. After a little while, the scene changed to Roy. He was standing on flat ground, but it looked like there was an earthquake. The ground was violently shaking and there were cracks almost everywhere I was able to see, except where Roy was standing. In the final part of my dream, I saw Lauren. She was in the middle of a huge forest with a lot of vegetation. There were two tall trees on either sides of her and other bushes, trees and flowers around her. The forest seemed calm at first, but then everything started growing rapidly, the stems and trunks started getting longer and thicker, spreading out in every direction possible, creating an arch over Lauren's head.

I woke up to the sound of Corvyre almost screaming at us to get up. Not exactly the most pleasant way to start the day. I walked over to the table and found some food waiting for us. It was the same as the day before: vegetables.

"Hooray, yummy grilled vegetables," said Roy sarcastically and unenthusiastically.

"Hooray," there was a unanimous groan.

When we finished eating, we walked to the training grounds and saw Corvyre waiting for us again.

"Today you will be tested on how long you can stay still without getting distracted," she said, "then, your reflexes will be tested and I will train you all according to how you did on these tests and the ones you did yesterday."

We were told to sit down, close our eyes and stay still. I had never been very good at sitting still, even though I don't have ADHD, my hands always need something to do. I can keep myself under control for a little while, but after that, I would burst. That was exactly what happened to me then. Naturally, I was the first one to stop. Next was Roy, then Alex, Xavier, and finally Lauren. I have to admit, I had never seen anyone stay focused as long as Lauren had, but I guess that's because I never bothered to see how long someone could sit still.

Next was the test of reflexes. Corvyre had a plant (that looked a lot like a cactus) sitting in a bowl of dirt. We were supposed to touch it and someone else would see how long it takes for our hands to pull away automatically.

"So, are we done here?" asked Roy while making hand motions as if he wanted to move on.

"Done? You're not done! This was merely the beginning! You are not even close to being almost halfway done!"

Chapter Three

"Dang it," said Roy.

"Well, you five can take an hour break, but you must come back here directly after you are done. Is that clear?"

"Yes," I said.

"Now that these tests are done, your training will indeed get started."

THE TRAINING BEGINS

Rick

"All right, I have five tasks for all of you" started Corvyre, "they might seem somewhat pointless at first, but you will soon realize the importance of them. You will come to your room inside the castle and you will see a piece of paper being held by two hooks in the ceiling: your job is to get the paper down to the ground without touching it, the walls, or the ceiling with anything. Next, you shall come back outside and you will find a log on the ground. You will have to set it on fire without using any tools. Your next task shall be to make a plant grow faster than it normally would, again, without any tools.

Then, you will go behind the castle and find a pond. Your job is to make a wave in the water without again without any equipment. Your final task will be to move a rock from one place to another without touching it. Each one of you can do one task and one task only. You are free to discuss how you will approach these tasks."

"Wait, but these are impossible! If we can't touch anything, how can we do them?" asked Alex.

"That is for you five to find out," replied Corvyre.

"Hey, I think I have an idea," I said, while thinking about the dream I had the night before.

"What is it?" Roy inquired.

"Okay, if you think about it, all of these tasks have to do with the elements, the only way to finish the first one would be to create a gust of wind. The only way to do the second one would be to instantaneously create a fire, the only way to do the third one would be to make the plant grow, the only way to do the fourth one would be to control the water, and the only way to do the last one would be to control the rock itself."

"That makes sense, but how will we know who can control which element and how?" asked Lauren.

The Training Begins

"Hold on, I'm getting to that," I said, "so, last night, I had a dream about us, it seemed like each one of us had a special power, I could control air, Alex could control fire, Xavier could control water, Roy could control earth, and Lauren could control plants."

"All right, since your dreams have been right before, I'll go with you on this one," said Xavier.

"Yeah, but we still have one problem," said Roy, "how will we suddenly learn how to control the elements?"

"Good question, but sadly, I don't have an answer," I said, my expression becoming doubtful, "I guess we'll just have to try."

We all spread out into the directions of where our tasks were, mine being in the castle. I walked over to our room and saw the piece of paper on the ceiling.

How am I supposed to control the air? I wondered.

I started by clearing my mind of everything except the air. I imagined it the way I saw it in my dream; a dark shade of white. I thought of the setting that my dream was in, but there were no living things. I imagined controlling the air, it became a part of me, it was pretty easy. But sadly, nothing happened in the real world. I tried the same thing, except this time, the setting was in our room. I imagined it the same way it actually looked, and when I started controlling the air, it felt the same way, but still, nothing happened.

I must be doing something wrong, I thought, *maybe if I imagine myself in there too, and if I do the same actions in real life.*

I tried it, but yet again, the same result. *Maybe what I'm doing wrong is that I don't have to imagine anything,* I thought to myself.

I opened my eyes and focused only on the air. After a little while, the air looked like it had in my dream. I moved my hands in the direction that I wanted the air to move in, and it responded. It had become a part of me. I took a small stream of air and gently pushed on one side of the paper. It had been so evenly placed that the moment the air pushed it, it fell straight down.

I caught the piece of paper and unrolled it, I expected something to be written on it, but it was completely blank.

The Training Begins

Alex

I walked up to the log and started thinking of ways I could create a fire. The first thing that came to my mind was to shout out "fire!" or "spark!", but it didn't work. The next thing I thought of doing was to close my eyes and think about the log on fire, but nothing happened. I came up with a lot of other ideas, but none of those worked either. I was about to give up just before a brilliant idea popped into my head.

I thought of a huge fire and focused on that in my head, then, I opened my hand with my palm facing up. Suddenly, my hand got hot, and I realized that I had created a small fire in my own hand! The only problem was that it was too hot and I couldn't control it. I created another fire in my hand, but this time, I was more focused on the fire in my hand rather than in my head. Because of the focus I had on the fire, I could control it a little. I lifted it up so that it wouldn't be too hot anymore. Once I was able to move the fire with more control over it, I made it jump out of my hand and into the air. I was surprised to see that it was still under my control. I could move it wherever I wanted it to go, but that was when I remembered the task I had to finish. I then gently dropped the fire onto the log, and it suddenly burst into flames. I realized that if the wind blew the fire far enough it would light the whole forest on fire.

I looked at the fire and focused as hard as I could, then, the fire became a part of me. I could make it do whatever I wanted, as if it were an extension of my body. I calmed it down and let the log slowly disintegrate into ashes.

Lauren

I stood there as everyone else departed to go to where their tasks were. "Corvyre," I started, "you didn't say where my task is."

"And which task would that be?"

"Making a plant grow faster."

"Ah, you must go to the forest and choose any plant you want, then tell me which one you have chosen."

Following Corvyre's directions, I walked over to the forest and chose a small, white flower. I told Corvyre that I had chosen it, and she walked back to the training grounds. The first way I decided that might make the plant grow was to make it grow, but that didn't work. I then realized that the only way for something to grow faster was if it got more energy. I tried to think of some places that the plant could get some excess energy from, but the only one I thought of was me. I tried many different ways to get my energy to flow to the plant, but only one worked.

First, I channeled all of my energy to my hands. Then, I closed my eyes and imagined the energy from my hands flowing to the plant through a gentle beam of energy that touched it. After I had the scene in my head, I opened my eyes, and the same thing was actually happening. When all the energy I had gathered was in the plant, its stem started shooting up. In the ten seconds that followed, it had grown at least six feet.

Once that was done, I almost couldn't stand up anymore. Because I had transferred so much of my own energy to the plant, there was barely enough to sustain me for very long. Realizing this, I walked over to Corvyre with the energy I still had.

Chapter Four

Xavier

I walked over to where Corvyre said there would be a pond, and guess what, there was. The first thing I noticed was the soft sound of the water moving with the wind. It was a very calming and peaceful sound. While still listening to the sound of the water, I thought of ways I could move the water. The first thing I tried was to move my hands in the way that I wanted the water to move, but nothing unnatural happened. Next, I tried blocking out the sound of the water and only focusing on what I wanted the water to do. There were many other things that I tried, but yet again, none of them worked.

I got tired of trying to move the water and just sat down. I then started to hear the sound of the water again, and I listened for a while before another idea popped into my head. The sound must be the key to moving the water. So then, I tried out my theory. I listened to the water and moved my hands in the way I wanted the water to move, but still, same result. Frustrated, I kicked a rock, but since the rock was planted firmly in the ground, I tripped. One hand went onto the ground and one hand went into the water. I got up, and my conscience told me to try one last time. I didn't think it would work, but it did. The water moved depending on how I moved my own hands. I couldn't figure out what I had done differently, but then, it hit me. I had to touch and hear the water to be completely in sync with it, so that I could move it. I started walking back feeling very proud of myself.

Roy

I started walking around looking for a rock that I could move, and I found one that was about one pound. I began by thinking about how the rock could magically lift up and start moving, but nothing came to mind. Since I couldn't think of anything, I found myself doing silly things, like trying to move it with my hands and eyes, throwing it in the air and seeing if it would just float, but nothing seemed to work. After a while, I started walking in circles around the rock to see if I could come up with any ideas, but I still couldn't.

I was frustrated, but I didn't want to give up. I sat down and started staring at the rock to see if it would help. I'm surprised to say that it actually did. I heard a sound come from a bird above me. I moved my eyes up to see what it was, but then I noticed that when I moved my eyes up or down, the rock did the same thing. The problem was, I could only move it up and down, and my task was to move it from one place to another. I wanted to see what would happen when I grabbed the rock, so I lifted my hand and moved it to where the rock was floating. But when my hand moved, the rock did the same. I had finally done it! I tried doing it a few more times, staring at it, lifting it with my eyes, and moving it with my hands. After a couple minutes of practice, I got pretty good. When I was satisfied with what I could do, I set the rock down and walked back to where Corvyre was.

Rick

I realized that if I just brought the paper to Corvyre, she might not believe that I had actually used the air to bring it down, so I let go of the paper and moved the air in such a way that it would set the paper right back onto the hooks.

I walked out of the castle and back to the training grounds where I saw everyone else walking back at the same time. When we all got there, Corvyre started talking, "Since you have come back, I assume you have all finished your task, correct?"

We all nodded.

"Good. Now I will follow each of you to your task, and you shall show me that you can actually do them. We will start with Rick, then Alex, Lauren, Xavier, and finally, Roy."

I motioned for everyone to follow me as I made my way into our room inside the castle. I looked up and saw that the paper was still sitting on the two hooks in the ceiling.

"Let's see what you can do!" said Alex with a huge smile across her face; as if she was challenging me.

I closed my eyes and remembered how the air had looked in my dream. I then opened my eyes and focused only on the air around me. After a short while, the air turned a dark shade of white. I started moving my hands, and the air responded. I made a small gust of wind that knocked the paper off the hooks and into my hands.

Chapter Four

Everyone immediately started clapping, then Corvyre told them to quiet down as she started talking, "Very well done Rick! Now Alex, show us the way."

Alex started walking after giving me look of approval with a hint of pride, soon took us back outside to where Corvyre had set up a log for her to burn. She stood there, motionless in front of the log, as if she were thinking about something. She then opened her palm upward, and a small flame appeared in it. The flame jumped out of her hand and onto the log, and as it slowly burned to ashes, we started clapping again.

Next, we followed Lauren into the forest. She led us to a white flower that was at least six feet tall.

"Wow," said Corvyre, "when Lauren chose to make this plant grow, it was no more than ten inches off the ground, and if you don't mind, can you make another one grow for us?"

"Sure, but since I used a lot of my energy to make that one grow, the next one won't get that much bigger."

Lauren turned her head to a tree and closed her eyes, then, a small ball of energy formed in her hands and went out to the tree. Almost instantly, the tree started growing, but after a few inches, it stopped. It was a sight to see.

"Now that, my friend," I said, "was pretty amazing."

"Thank you," she responded.

We then started walking over to the pond: where Xavier was supposed to make a wave without touching it. First, he stood there, waiting for what he said was the sound of the water. Next, he dipped his hand into the water and walked back a few steps. He then started moving his hands, and the water did the same thing. Soon enough, the pond had waves in it, it was pretty impressive.

After that was done, we headed over to where Roy had learned to move rocks. He picked up a somewhat small rock and showed it to us. He then put it back on the ground and focused only on it. Then, he moved his eyes up and so did the rock. When it was just floating in air, he moved his left hand to the right side, and the rock followed whatever his hand did. He set it down in front of Corvyre, and she looked impressed.

"Good, now that you can each control an element, I must tell you something."

Chapter Four

"What is it?" Roy asked suddenly.

"Have patience. Now, I must tell you that you cannot do much with the elements because you do not posses the orbs. These orbs are very powerful and can be dangerous if they fall into the wrong hands. There is one for each element, air, fire, water, earth, plants, and lightning. With the orbs, a person can store either energy or some of the element itself in them. You can use this energy at any time you need it, and it can be very helpful in battle. There are six in all, and one of them has already fallen into the wrong hands."

"Let me guess," said Xavier, "it's lightning, because none of us can control that element."

"Correct. And lightning is the most powerful weapon, the only way someone that can control lightning can be defeated is if all the other elements work together."

"Wait, then who has it?" I asked, confused.

"Kevdak has informed me that it is in the possession of the foxes at this point, but I do not know what they are doing with it, because none of the animals can control the elements. Anyways, the other five orbs are hidden; even we do not know where they are. Not too long ago, a human named Aric Johnson was in this world. He was about the only human we have ever trusted, and he could understand us because his ancestors knew our language and it was passed down from generation to generation. He could also control all six elements. At that point in time, the orbs were in our possession, and we lent them to him. But while the entire village was sleeping, the foxes managed to get inside a room where we kept one of the orbs. Sadly, we found out too late that they were here. They had already found the orb and were trying to find the others, so we told Aric to get the other orbs and hide them. He hid them far away from our kingdom, and before he got a chance to tell us where the orbs are, the foxes forced him to flee into your world. Now that he is dead, there is only one person who knows their exact locations; his daughter: Eve Johnson."

"Wait a second, did you say *Eve Johnson*?" I asked.

"Yes, I did indeed, why do you ask?"

"Because we know an Eve Johnson whose father is now dead and his name was Aric, and I don't think that's a coincidence," I responded.

Chapter Four

"Okay, well since you claim to know this person, you must go look for her, but not now. You must first be trained to use weapons."

"Awesome!" yelled Roy, "what kind of weapons?"

"You, Rick and Alex will be using swords, and Lauren and Xavier will be using bows and arrows,"

"Cool! When do we start?" asked Alex.

"Tomorrow. Your training is done for today."

The rest of the day was like the day before, nothing else that was exciting or important happened, just a regular old day. Not even my dream was important that night, but I think it had something to do with those orbs that Corvyre had described.

The next morning, we didn't have to wake up as early as the day before, so I think I got enough sleep to get me through the day. When we got ready, we walked outside to the training grounds where we found Corvyre waiting for us with some weapons sitting on the ground.

"Hello," she said, "you got a good night's sleep, yes?"

"Yes," we all moaned.

The Training Begins

"Good, then you will be ready to train with your weapons. First, I will have you each carry a weapon and see which one fits you best."

Xavier and Lauren grabbed bows and that seemed their sizes while Roy, Alex and I tried out the swords. The cross-guards on all of the swords (for all of you who don't know what a cross-guard is, it's the thing that separates the hilt from the blade) were pointed towards the tip of the blade, rather than being completely straight out or downwards. I pick up the shortest sword I could see. It felt awkward because it was a bit too light, so I picked the next size. None of them felt right, until I got to the second heaviest one, I was surprised that it was the one that felt right to me. Alex's was one of the lighter ones and Roy's was about average in weight. As I was examining how the swords looked, I noticed that there were small, fist-sized indents on the hilts of all the swords that looked the same size.

I looked over to see how Lauren and Xavier were doing, and saw that Lauren's bow and arrow was a bit bigger than Xavier's. The designs on the bows were very elaborate, and the arrows looked well made too. I noticed that right above the place where you would put an arrow, there was also a small indent that seemed the same size as on the swords.

"Now that you have all found a weapon of your size, we will start the training," stated Corvyre.

"One quick question," I said, "why are there small indents on all the weapons?"

"You are very observant, Rick. These weapons were specially foraged to fit the orbs. After you get your orb and it is placed into your weapon, something different will happen to each of your weapons depending on the element of the orb."

"Oh. Well good to know," I said.

"First, you will learn the correct posture, then you will learn all the techniques you will need. Finally, the swordsmen will duel each other and archers will shoot at small targets I have set up in the forest.

"I will first give instructions to the swordsmen. Okay, put the sword in your dominant hand."

All three of us were right-handed, so it made it easier for Corvyre to give us instructions.

The Training Begins

"If you are right-handed, put your right foot back, bend your knees a little and turn a little to the right. While doing this, you must keep you head facing forward, your sword hand out and your sword tilted forward a small bit."

We did what she said, and I found myself in a fighting stance that actually felt like a natural position to fight in.

"Now, to make an accurate underhand swing, step forward with your left foot and swing your right arm in an arc from bottom to top. Once you can do this action correctly, try it in real time until you get the feel for it."

I did the action a couple times slowly, until I finally figured out the exact movements, I then started to do it "in real time" until the action came almost naturally.

"Next, you will do the same action with your feet, but you will swing your arm from one side to another. After you can do this, then try an overhand swing, they are usually done with two hands and very powerfully. Now, I must go to help the archers. I will check up on you to see how much progress you've made after they have the correct techniques."

Chapter Four

I tried the side swing slowly until I got the feel for it, and then started doing an overhand. After a little while, I started to do the moves as I would in a real battle.

It seemed Corvyre was done with teaching Xavier and Lauren, so she walked back over to where we were practicing. "All right, first, Roy will fight Rick, and the winner will fight Alex. After that, Alex and Roy will fight and the winner will fight Rick, finally, Alex will be against Rick and the winner will be fighting Roy. Got it?"

"Yes," I said, "but how do we know who wins?"

"When one person falls or they have a sword pointed at their face, the one still standing is the winner. Oh, and I forgot to tell you, no hurting each other, this is only practice."

"Okay," I said, ready to fight.

Roy and I faced each other in our stances; Corvyre said "Go!" and left. I looked at Roy, ready to swing my sword at him, but he beat me to it. I parried his blow with another swing, and our swords made a loud *clang* as they collided. I put both hands on the hilt so that I would have more power, and I pushed Roy's sword down with one massive burst of energy. I took a step back and got into my stance while remembering Corvyre telling us not to hurt each other. If it had been real, I would have done much more than that. When Roy got back into his stance, I swung my sword at him and he blocked it. This kept going on for a while, and I didn't think anyone would win, but my hands started getting really sweaty because I was getting tired.

Roy swung his sword at me one last time, I tried to block it, but I didn't have enough grip to hold on, so the sword flew out of my hand. Seeing that, Roy pointed his sword at my neck, and I knew I had lost. It was fine though, because I think I had put up a pretty good fight.

Next, it was Roy and Alex fighting. When they got in their stances, I yelled "Go!" like Corvyre had. Alex and Roy kept swinging their swords while the other person blocked it. The fight became somewhat boring because the two of them were so evenly matched. Finally, Alex tried a new technique, while Roy was swinging his sword from the side, Alex put her sword under Roy's and twisted her hand so that her sword went on top and Roy's was twisted out of his hand. Alex pointed his sword at Roy, and the match was over.

Chapter Four

"Now I guess you two fight again," I said, remembering Corvyre's instructions.

"Only this time, I'll win!" said Roy.

"You sure about that?" asked Alex with a sly smile on her face.

"Oh, I'm sure."

They got into their stances again, and started fighting at my command. The fight went on the same way, except, like Roy had said, the outcome would be different. Alex tried to disarm him again, but Roy countered it by pushing the blade downwards when it was right above Alex's. Caught by surprise, Alex's sword was pushed straight out of her hand. Roy then pointed the sword at Alex's neck, so Roy was the winner.

Next, it was me against Roy. I got ready, and at Alex's mark, we started. Most of it was like all other fights, swing, block swing, block, and the pattern repeated. A while into the fight, I had an idea, instead of blocking Roy's swings by putting my blade in front of his, why not block it by hitting his sword back? I started doing what I had thought about, and eventually, my swings got so powerful, that it knocked Roy's sword out of his hand, and I won.

"Only two fights left," I said, exhausted.

I faced Alex in my stance and when Roy told us to start, I swung my sword from the side. She tried to do that disarming maneuver she had figured out, but when her sword was coming up, I pushed mine the other way and got back in my stance. Fighting Alex was harder than fighting Roy. She did an overhand swing, I blocked it, but the force she had put in the swing knocked me down onto one knee. I had my sword in front of my face being pushed back at me by Alex's sword, and since she was standing, she could put her body's weight into the sword, whereas I only had the strength of my arms. I guess that was actually a lot of power because I was able to get up and push Alex down. When she was on the ground, I pulled my sword back as if swinging it at her, but instead, used her own technique against her.

"I won!" I shouted, while throwing my hands in the air.

The final match was me against Roy, and I had already fought twice in a row, so I knew I would lose.

Chapter Four

"Wait," I said as we were just about to start, "can I have a two minute break or something?"

"Hey, I fought three matches in a row and I didn't get a break, so you shouldn't either," Roy complained.

"All right, no break for me then," I said, tired and disappointed.

"Go!" shouted Alex, and we began the final match. I started by swinging from below, but Roy blocked it. I then swung from the side and Roy tried the disarming maneuver. I countered it, but he kept hold of his sword. I did an overhand strike, but Roy blocked it again. I tried another underhand blow, and he blocked it. We kept our swords there, pushing against each other, but my sword slipped, and all of my power pushed the sword up to the cross-guard of his, and the blade was trapped, unless I pulled it back to me, which I did. Then I realized something: since the blade had been trapped, if I moved my blade, wouldn't his move with mine? I tested out my theory. I did another underhand swing, and Roy blocked it, which was good for me. I then slid the blade of my sword up to the cross-guard of his, and made sure it was trapped inside. I pushed the blade back, and to the side, and, as I had thought, his blade came out of his hand. I had won three matches in a row!

Just then, Corvyre walked over. "So," she said, "what have you learned?"

"Well," I started, "we learned this disarming technique that Alex figured out, and Roy figured out how to counter it, I started blocking by hitting the other person's sword, and I can disarm people with their cross-guard."

Corvyre then called Xavier and Lauren over to where we were standing. "Very well done, you five," she said, "your training is done for the day. You may spend the rest of the day how you like. Tomorrow, you will continue training with weapons."

"So," said Alex while we started walking away, "what should we do for the rest of the day?"

"I have an idea!" I said, remembering the day before.

"What is it?" asked Roy.

"You know how yesterday, Corvyre was telling us about those orbs, and how only one person knows where they are?"

"Yeah, what about it?" Xavier asked.

Chapter Four

"Well, since we know the person who knows the location of all the orbs, and we have nothing to do today, why not go back to Danville and ask Eve to tell us where they are, so we don't have to do it later?"

"That's a good idea. Let's tell Corvyre what we're going to do," said Lauren.

We turned around and ran over to Corvyre, "We've decided to go back to our world and find out where the orbs are from our friend," said Lauren.

"That would be very helpful, but you will be back by tomorrow, yes?" she asked.

"Oh, yeah, definitely," I said.

"Good, then you will not miss your training tomorrow morning, but if you do, I will be very upset with the five of you."

"Okay, see you tomorrow," I said.

We had all kept our weapons with us for some reason, and we headed back to where we remembered the portal was, and saw that it was there, glowing, just like it had been before. We took turns going into the bush, and back into our own world.

WE MEET A FRIEND

Rick

I stepped out of the bush, and back onto Wolf Mountain. It felt nice being back in Danville. I had been so used to talking in the animals' language, I almost started talking in it instead of in English, "So, anyone know Eve's address?"

"Um, I think I do," said Roy, "I'll lead the way there."

Since Roy had so confidently said he knew the way, we followed him. We went down the mountain, and almost half an hour had passed before we reached the bottom. We followed Roy into the neighborhood across from mine, and then went onto a street I had never been on before. When we finally reached the house Roy thought was Eve's, I rang the doorbell.

Eve's house was at the end of a street, and there was only one street connecting to her street, and that was on the opposite side. There were about twelve houses in all on the street, and they were all two story houses. The neighborhood that she lived in was (luckily) not gated; otherwise, we wouldn't have been able to get in. The small spots of grass that separated one house from another, were mostly dead. I guess that tells you about people's view towards nature.

"Who is it?" I heard from inside.

"It's Rick, Roy, Xavier, Alex, and Lauren," I said.

The door opened, and Eve was standing in the doorway. She has dark hair that goes a little past her shoulders, and light skin. She's a bit taller than me, which I always hated, and was wearing a red t-shirt and jeans, but for some reason, she looked shocked.

"What are you guys doing here? And why do you all have dangerous weapons?" she asked.

We Meet a Friend

"I'll explain later," I said, "and what do you mean, are we not supposed to be here?"

"No, I mean you five left almost two weeks ago and have been missing ever since! Your parents even called the police, and they sent out a search team, it's been all over the news! You had disappeared off the face of the Earth! Where were you?!"

"It'll all make sense soon, but can we come in?"

"I think it's all right, my mom is gone for the week on a business trip, so it'll be safe for you."

"Great," I said, as we walked inside. We went into the living room and all sat down on the couches.

"You have some explaining to do," said Eve.

"Yes, I know," I said.

"Then get to it!"

"All right, fine, don't have to be pushy," I said, with my hands in front of me, "okay, so this is our story, by the way, it's completely true. First off, I have to tell you that there's another world that is parallel to ours, called Neosolgis, and there are no humans, only animals. The animals can talk to each other, and somehow, the five of us know their language. Before we went to Neosolgis,

97

there was a kingdom ruled by wolves, but then invaders came and captured the king.

"Okay, now I have to tell you that there are these six orbs that let you control the elements, and you can only use them if you can already control that element. The elements are fire, water, air, earth, plants, and lightning. Lightning is the most powerful element and the only way to defeat someone that can control it is if the other five elements come together and defeat them. Right now, the invaders, who are the foxes, have the lightning orb, and that's why nobody can overpower them."

"Wait, but if the other five orbs haven't been stolen, why can't you just use those to beat the foxes?"

"Because," said Lauren, "the other orbs haven't been stolen, but hidden, and only one person knows where they are. Do you have any idea who this person is?"

"Not really…" she said, looking confused.

"It's you."

"But, how should I know where these orbs are?"

"The wolves told us that your dad was able to control all six elements," I started, "but one night, the foxes sneaked in and stole the lightning orb. Your dad was then instructed to hide the other orbs, which he did, but before he got a chance to tell the wolves where they are, the foxes forced him back into this world. He then came and told you where the five orbs are, and soon died."

"Well, my dad did disappear a lot, but he would never tell us why, and I'm actually not sure if he's dead, once, he left and he hasn't come back since. But he did give me five maps, even though they don't make any sense because I can't find out the areas they were referring to."

"Great," I said, "can you give them to us?"

"Not so fast, my dad also told me never to give the maps to anyone unless I am one hundred percent sure that they are the good guys and are in desperate need of them," she responded.

"But how can we prove to you that we're actually the good guys?" I asked.

"That's for you to figure out."

"Hey, I know," said Xavier, "we could take her to Neosolgis, talk to the wolves and have the wolves convince her that we're the good guys!"

"Why can't we do it ourselves?" asked Lauren.

Chapter Five

"The wolves would have proof that we need the orbs," Alex suggested.

"I guess we're going then," I said, "Okay Eve, before we take you, I need to ask, did your dad ever teach you the language of the animals?"

"Yes, he did, why?"

"Because you are going to talk to some animals," I said.

"Okay, when do we leave?"

"As soon as possible," I said, "but before we go, can we get something to eat? I'm really hungry, and I think everyone else is too."

Eve went into her kitchen and came back a few minutes later with some cookies in six different plastic bags, and six bottles of water.

"Why is everything packaged?" asked Alex.

"Because," said Eve, "you're eating while we walk."

We went out the door as Eve handed each of us a bottle of water and a bag of cookies. Roy led the way, again. We walked over to Wolf Mountain and had to hike up, to me, it felt like the billionth time I had been there. It took about an hour to get all the way back to the portal, and by that time, everyone was only carrying an empty water bottle and a plastic bag.

"So, what do we do now?" asked Eve.

"We go to the giant bush," I responded.

"What giant bush?" she asked, looking very confused.

"The giant bush is the portal between the two worlds, and it is the only portal in the world." said Lauren.

"Okay, so, what do we do, walk through the bush?"

"Yes, indeed we do," I stated.

We walked over to the bush and all went through it; Eve was last. When we got to the other side, Eve looked and sounded amazed, "My dad used to tell me stories about this place, but I never thought that it actually existed!"

"Well, you better believe it, because here we are," I said.

"Hey," said Alex, "let's go find Kevdak or Corvyre and see if they can convince Eve."

"Good thinking, let's go," I said.

We walked over to the castle and found Corvyre sitting outside, "What are you doing here?" she asked, "I thought you went to get the locations of the orbs. Are you finished already?"

"No, we're not finished, Eve doesn't believe that we're the good guys, so she won't give us the locations, and we need you to convince her."

"Okay, I will try my best to convince her, but I must talk to her privately."

"All right, let's go," I said.

We walked inside the castle and into our room, where we sat on our beds and did just about nothing. After about an hour had passed, Corvyre and Eve walked into the room.

"Okay, I'm not one hundred percent convinced that you're the good guys yet, so, I've decided to give you the locations of only four of the orbs, and when you bring them back to me and prove to me that you are using them for good, somehow, then I will give you the location of the fifth one."

"It's a deal," I said while shaking her hand.

We walked out of the castle and back to the portal, for the second time that day. What I was really dreading was going down the mountain again. When we got to the portal, I was the first one to go through. I got to the other side and immediately started walking down Wolf Mountain. Everyone else followed me silently, almost like a shadow. I remembered the way we had followed Roy to Eve's house, and went the same way. When we got there, Eve took a key out of her pocket and let us all inside.

She led us into the living room and started to talk, "You guys stay here, I have to go find the maps. They're in a special place."

Eve walked away and came back a few minutes later holding four big, old, brown pieces of paper that each had a map of Neosolgis and different location on each of them. Also, written across the top, there was the element of the orb that each map would lead to. Eve laid them out on the floor and all of us grabbed the one that had our element on it. Everyone had one, except Lauren.

"Sorry Lauren," said Eve, "I picked a random one not to give to you , so, I guess you're not going to find your orb very soon."

"It's okay, I'll be fine," she responded.

"We won't get our orbs that soon either," I said.

Chapter Five

"Why not?" Eve inquired.

"Because, Corvyre says we still need to train more before we're ready to go and find the orbs and rescue King Olkin."

"Oh, I see."

I looked down at the map and saw that my orb was hidden at the highest point of the tallest mountain in the region that was shown.

"Your dad probably has these places pretty well protected," said Lauren.

"Yeah, he didn't want anyone to find them, especially by mistake," said Eve.

"All right, we had better get going," I said.

"Hope nothing happens to you guys," said Eve.

"Yeah, so do I," said Xavier.

With that, all five of us walked out the door with the maps in our hands. We had gone the path to Wolf Mountain enough times, and I was getting tired of it. Either way, I had to keep going. We walked out of the neighborhood and to the mountain. When we got there, we decided to take a twenty minute break so that we would all have enough energy to climb up.

We Meet a Friend

In those twenty minutes, I had decided to take a good look at my map so that I would know where to go. I started by looking at the castle, and saw that the mountain my orb was hidden on was south of it. I would have to follow a winding trail through a forest to get to the mountain. Then, I would have to climb up the mountain. I thought I was being smart by thinking I could just climb up another side of the mountain, but I soon saw that the map showed that there was only one way to the summit. It turns out that Eve's father was smarter than me.

After I was done, I glanced at my watch and realized that twenty minutes were over. "Let's get going," I said, while starting to stand up.

"Okay," said Roy reluctantly.

We started hiking up the mountain, and got to the top about forty-five minutes later. Lauren walked over to the pond, bent down, and started drinking some water. It seemed like a good idea, so I walked over and did the same. Soon enough, all five of us were all drinking water.

After about five minutes, we were all finished, and we walked over to the portal.

Chapter Five

"Hey, did anyone else notice how we can pass through the portal at any time we want now?" asked Alex, seeming very curious.

"Now that I think about it, it is kind of weird," I said.

"Do you have an explanation for it?"

"I…" I paused to think, "Have no idea."

"Maybe we can ask Kevdak when we get there, I mean, he is the guardian of the portal, right?" said Xavier.

"That's a great idea," said Lauren.

"What are we waiting for?" I asked impatiently, "Let's go!"

With that, we all stepped into the portal, and came out in the other world. I was expecting to see the fresh, green grass and the healthy forest, as we always had, but I saw that entire place was on fire. Of course our first instinct was a panic attack and natural human response to run away from the huge blazing trees facing us, then, I had an idea to save the forest. "Hey Alex!" I shouted over the crackling of fire and the burning of wood.

"Yeah?" she responded.

We Meet a Friend

"Do you think that you can calm this fire down by controlling it?!" I asked while dodging a falling tree trunk.

"I'm not sure, but it's worth a shot!" Alex shouted back at me.

"Hey, anyone else find it ironic that it's not Mr. Blaze here that can control fire?" Roy asked jokingly.

"Now's not the time for jokes, Roy!" I shouted.

Alex focused only on the fire, and started moving her free hand, but the fire still moved as wildly as before. "It's no use!" she shouted, "It won't respond to me!"

"Why not?" I asked.

"How should I know?!" she asked, seeming very frustrated.

"Let's go to the castle and find Corvyre or Kevdak!" shouted Lauren, "They should know what to do!"

We started running through the blazing forest, making sure that none of us would catch on fire. When we were able to see the castle, I thought it would be normal there, but obviously, it wasn't. In the distance, I saw a teenage boy, maybe thirteen or fourteen, shooting bolts of lightning from his hands at the castle, wolves, or at trees.

He had blond hair, and since I was far away, I couldn't tell much else about him. I wondered if he had set the forest on fire and how one person alone could do so much damage.

As soon as we realized that the castle was under attack, we ran down as fast as we could to see what we could do to help. When we got there, the first wolf I saw was Kevdak. "Who's attacking the castle and why?" I asked him.

"From what I know, his name is Bailey," said Kevdak.

"But why is he attacking?" inquired Lauren

"We believe he is working with the foxes, and that he possesses the lightning orb," he responded.

"Well, now we know what the foxes are using it for," said Xavier.

"How can we help?" I asked, feeling kind of scared because of what Corvyre had told us about the lightning orb.

"Go inside the castle to your room and you will find your weapons on your beds."

"All right, let's go," I said.

We Meet a Friend

We ran inside the castle and into our room as fast as we could to get our weapons. I grabbed my sword, and put down the map in its place. I saw that there was also a sheath for the sword and a belt to tie around my waist. I put it on then turned around and saw that the others had done the same thing. Lauren and Xavier had their bows and arrows in a pouch slung across their backs. Roy and Alex had their swords in their sheaths and were ready to go.

"Let's rock and roll," I said, feeling much more confident than I had been before.

As we walked outside, I felt as if we were in some kind of epic action movie, but I guess anyone would have in my position. We approached Kevdak, and he started talking. "Good, now, you will be able to fight. I'm not sure what you three with swords can do right now, but with the bows and arrows; try to shoot the boy that is destroying the castle."

THE ATTACK

Bailey

I aimed my hand at their castle, and a small jolt or electricity left me. I looked to the side of the castle and saw three boys and two girls, three with swords, and two with bows. *Those must be the kids that the king had told me about,* I thought. My orders had been to capture them, alive, and take them back to the king. Just then, the one holding the bow with brown hair raised his weapon and shot an arrow straight at me, but I shot it with lightning and it exploded right in front of my eyes. *Those imbeciles, do they really think they can defeat me?! I am in control of the element of lightning! The only way they can win is if they already have their orbs, like me, but that is impossible for some of such inferior skill,* I thought.

Soon after, the boy and the girl with bows started rapidly shooting at me, but of course, all of them either missed or got blown to bits. I realized that I might soon need my sword, so I took it out of its sheath that was slung across my back. At the bottom of the hilt was the orb, it had looked as if it had electricity inside of it, but that was because I had been saving it for almost a whole year. It had charged the entire sword with lightning, so it looked electrified and only I was able to hold it. As both of them shot arrows at once, the other three started running at me. Both of the arrows were about to hit me, but I zapped them and they exploded in front of me, blinding me for a second.

In that time, the other three came in front of me and started slashing their swords with the most basic of techniques. I dodged all of their swings, but I figured that three against one was not a fair match, so I shouted "Go!" and pointed my sword at them. They all fell back, screaming in pain as they were getting scratched by invisible forces.

"What's happening?!" I heard one shout.

"It must be some kind of mind power! And it's painful!" screamed another.

"Xavier! Lauren! Help us!" the last one shouted at the top of his lungs.

Just after, the two with bows, probably called Lauren and Xavier, shot arrows at me, but went on either sides of me. I didn't have time to blow them up, so one of the worst possible things happened. My partner was shot. The second it happened, she became visible, and so did my army.

"I thought you were protecting me!" she shouted, her arm bleeding.

"I did my best, now stop complaining and get them all invisible again!" I shouted, feeling very angry.

"I only have enough strength to hide one object, and I would prefer that to be myself."

"Fine, go back and get yourself healed. But then you must come back here as soon as possible," I said, and with that, she vanished.

The Attack

"There's a fox attacking me!" said boy with black hair.

"Well, obviously! We can see them now!" said the boy with dark brown hair.

They started attacking the foxes with their swords as I commanded the entire army of foxes behind me to take down their beloved caste and destroy anything that came in the way. The foxes then scattered and started destroying everything. It was perfect; just as I had planned.

At the same time, the two girls and three boys were fighting off at least five foxes each. They were hopelessly outnumbered and clearly outmatched. It seemed like they realized it when one yelled, "We can't keep this up for much longer! The only way to survive is to flee!"

"Then everyone will think we're wimps!" shouted the one with black hair and a sword.

"Would you rather die?!"

"No. Fine, let's go."

After that, they ran off. *I have no choice but to pursue them because if I got back without the boys, Lord Shaeak would have me killed. Well, probably not something of that extreme because I am his right-hand man,* I thought, *but I might get tortured for disobeying him.* I then sheathed my sword and started to follow them.

They ran past the castle and into the flaming forest. *Those fools,* I thought, *they're going to get themselves killed, but that would be less work for me.*

They ran over to a colossal bush and started talking amongst themselves, but I was unable to hear what they were saying over the burning of the forest, and because I was too far away. As I was walking closer, they tried to speed up their conversation, sadly, they succeeded. As soon as I got about ten feet away from them, their conversation was over.

I took my sword out of its sheath, and one of the boys walked inside the bush, but didn't go out the other side. I found that quite unusual, but I didn't have time to ponder over it because the three boys with swords came charging at me. They stared swinging their swords at me, but I kept blocking them by sending electric shocks through their swords, therefore shocking them.

"He's too strong!" the one with light hair shouted.

The Attack

"What can we do?" another shouted while trying to dodge my blow.

"Xavier! Distract him by shooting some arrows! Alex, Roy you two try to disarm him while I go get something from the castle!"

"Rick!" shouted the one called Xavier.

"What?"

"Be careful!"

"I will, and you too!"

With that, the one who was apparently named Rick ran off. I tried to stop him, but I would have gotten myself killed by the other three. Xavier shot an arrow at me, but I didn't try to destroy it because I wouldn't fall for the same trick twice. I simply moved to the side and dodged the arrow. In that time, Alex and Roy tried attacking me by surprise. It didn't work at all; I was completely expecting it. I blocked both of their swords at the same time, and sent a shock through them.

I then sent a small, but powerful bolt of white and blue lightning at Xavier. The second I sent lightning at him, he shot an arrow so that the arrow would get demolished, instead of him. He seemed smarter than I thought, but it was probably just luck.

In the time that I had just bought myself, I ran deeper into the forest. Not to hide or run away, because only someone who needed to would do that. No, I had gone in the forest to protect myself and defeat the other three boys. When they realized I had gone into the forest, Xavier started shooting arrows at me, but they all missed because he was too busy avoiding falling trees and flames. The other two ran at me with their swords, but I kept going behind trees or blocking their attacks. After a short period of time, the trees started to get so weak, that when Alex and Roy would hit one with their swords, they would fall over, backwards.

The two of them were bringing their own doom. As trees kept falling on them, they would move out of the way, but I knew that some time, the tree wouldn't miss them. I started running even deeper into the forest when I remembered what Lord Shaeak had told me about the orbs. I had to kill all five of the boys together, and then destroy the orbs quickly, or the orbs would find new owners and become invincible again. It was then that I came up with a master plan that I was sure would work, but, I can't reveal it just yet.

I pretended to run into a tree, drop my weapon, and become unconscious. I closed my eyes, fell on the ground, and the three boys ran over to me.

"Should we kill him while we have a chance?" asked Roy.

"We should wait and ask Rick first," answered Xavier, "and help me lift him so we can bring him to the castle."

"But what about his sword?" asked Alex.

"Roy," said Xavier, "find a rock and pick up the sword with it because we can't without getting electrocuted. Then put it on top of him to make it easier for all of us."

I don't know exactly what happened after that, but I soon felt the cold blade of my sword against my chest. The next thing I knew, two people were carrying me by the feet and one person by my head. It was really hurting me, and really wanted to get up and walk there myself, but I knew I couldn't do that.

Chapter Six

After a few minutes of them carrying me, they set me down on what I think was a bed. Then, they started talking. "Hey," said Rick, "nice job, you got him. Now, to make sure he doesn't escape, let's put him in some chains I got."

"I have a question," said Roy, "why can't we just kill him? It would save us a lot of trouble."

"Because," said Rick," for one, we are *not* killers, and two, he might have a lot of useful information."

"Okay, so what do we do with him?"

"That's what I haven't thought about yet."

"Let's put him in the chains before he becomes conscious again!" shouted Xavier.

They then put the chains around every part of my body, except my head, but luckily, the chains around my arms were loose enough for me to move them. That would help my plan. Also, since they couldn't touch my sword, they had no choice but to leave it on top of me. The orb in my sword would also help me because I wouldn't be able to do much without it, and if I was too far away from it, the power stored inside of it would be useless to me.

The Attack

A few minutes after they tied the chains around me, I decided that it was time for my plan to go in action. I slowly opened my eyes and sat up on the bed. I heard a faint sound; it was like clawing and tearing of something. I then knew they had taken me inside their castle. The room in which I was in was small. There were five beds, and a wooden table in the middle. The room had six walls, one for each bed and one for the door. I was sitting on one bed and the other four beds were occupied by Xavier, Alex, Roy, and Rick.

"Why were you destroying the castle?!" screamed Rick.

I answered him, but I only told part of the truth. I was not allowed to reveal anything, or the entire plan would be endangered. "Because I had to," I said.

"You will have to answer our questions or we will never let you go," said Xavier.

Fools, I thought, *they think I cannot escape? This has been an act! I could escape now if I wanted to! I can kill them all too!*

"Okay," I said, "but know this: once you let me go, I will show no mercy on you, or the wolves!"

Chapter Six

"We know that you work with the foxes, so you have to know the location of King Olkin," said Rick.

"I do not," I said, untruthfully.

"Liar!" shouted Alex while standing up.

Between all of the questions they were asking me, I was thinking about when the right time to break free would be. The time came when they were done asking questions and were about to take me to "jail," as they called it.

I stood up and slipped my arms out of the chains. I then made a small ball of lightning between my hands; I was getting the power from the orb. I put the ball in my chest and felt the electricity running through my entire body. I looked down and saw that my legs had blue and white bolts of lightning around them. The same thing was happening all over my body, except for my head. The lightning hit the chains, and they exploded. I was free, and the four of them looked terrified.

I started walking towards them while creating another ball of electricity in my hands. Then, Rick started talking. "We have to go get the orbs! Now!"

The Attack

They each grabbed a brown, rolled up piece of parchment and their weapons and ran out the door. I grabbed my sword and went after them. When everyone was outside the castle, which wasn't much of a castle anymore because of what my army had done to it, they all started running in different directions. I knew I couldn't chase them all, so I didn't. I didn't even chase one of them because for my master plan to work, they all needed to find their orbs first. Everything was going according to plan.

I looked around and saw how much damage my army and I had done. The place used to be beautiful, but it was in ruins when I was done with it. The forest that was next to the castle had just finished burning. There were only fallen trees, burned tree stumps and frightened animals. The ground was entirely covered in ashes. All I had done was throw a lightning bolt at one tree, and I saw how much damage I had done. It made me realize how much one thing could effect much more than just itself.

Since those boys were out finding their orbs, I decided to stay back and keep destroying the castle because I had nothing better to do. *They are so predicable; falling right into my trap. This time, they will definitely get themselves killed,* I thought.

I looked over at the castle and saw that my foxes were still taking it down. It was scratched almost everywhere, and the stones were wearing down badly. Once the stones were worn down enough, it would be easy for the foxes to break through the walls. If that was to happen, the wolves would have no chance of surviving. Then, the only thing standing in the way of us ruling the world would be those foolish boys that I would soon dispose of.

I stood there, staring at their castle while observing my foxes' tactics. They were clawing at the castle weakly. I walked over to one of them to see what was wrong.

"Sir," said one of them as it turned to me and bowed its head in respect, "the walls are thick and we are all getting tired. May we take a break?"

I stood there for a little while, thinking. *If I let them take a break, it would give the wolves a chance to get an army ready, but, if the foxes keep going for much longer, they might faint, I won't have an army at all. I guess a break is the best solution,* I thought.

The Attack

"Fine," I said, "you may take a break to get your strength back."

When I finished my sentence, they all started cheering and stopped doing whatever they were doing. I started walking, and the foxes started following me. I led them to the forest, and soon realized that the forest wasn't there anymore, and that meant there would be nothing I could get the foxes to eat. I looked to my left side and saw small trees in the distance. Apparently there was still a part of the forest that hadn't gotten burned.

I then turned around and shouted, "Come with me! There might be food in another part of the forest!"

The foxes kept following me obediently. I walked past lots of burned tree stumps and charred trees lying on the ground. As I looked closely, there also appeared to be burrows for animals that used to live there. *Imagine all of the homes of the poor helpless animals that were ruined,* I thought, *but, who cares, doesn't affect me.*

I kept walking for a while, and finally came to the part of the forest that was still alive. There were trees everywhere and animals running around; getting food and such. I kept walking and got to an opening in the forest with a bunch of berry bushes. There were small, round and light blue berries on them. Those berries were not found almost anywhere in the world.

"Here you go," I said while directing the foxes to the bushes. The hungry army of about one hundred rushed to the bushes and started eating as much they could in as little time as possible. I decided that I was hungry, so I walked over to the least crowded bush and picked a few berries off.

I walked back to where I was initially, sat down, and started eating. I had nothing to do, so I looked around. In the circular clearing of the forest, there were many berry bushes in the middle, enough to feed an entire army. Well, my army anyways. Other than that, there was green grass all over the ground and trees around the edges that towered above everything else. The sky was bright blue and the sun shined as brightly as possible, beating down on my face. It was near the middle of the sky, so I knew what time it was.

When I finished my berries, I went over to one of the bushes and got some more. My foxes weren't eating berries anymore, so I assumed that they were finished.

The Attack

They were all roaming around the bushes, waiting for me to finish. I then walked to a tree, sat down and calmly ate my berries.

"Let us go!" I announced as I consumed my last berry.

I started walking back the way we came, and my army followed me. After a few minutes of walking through a beautiful forest, I saw the burned part of the forest. It most certainly wasn't as pretty, but it was easier to navigate because there were no giant trees blocking the way. I turned to my right and saw the ruined castle with small specks lined up in front of it. It was very far away, so I couldn't tell what they were.

I then remembered that the five boys had escaped, and to make it easier for me later, I decided to let them find their orbs, but get wounded so they would be easy to kill. I walked over to one of my most trusted warriors, and told him to go after the five boys one by one and injure them after they find their orbs. "Go after the one called Rick first. I think he is their leader, without him, they will all be helpless."

Chapter Six

As I led my army closer, I could finally tell what was standing in front of the castle, it was as I had suspected. There was an army of wolves.

THE MOST POWERFUL PERSON IN THE WORLD WANTS TO KILL US

Rick

We ran into the flaming forest (that would have sounded like a cool forest name, if it hadn't been literal) and found the portal. I turned around to see that the guy whose name was Bailey was still following us. We ran through a lot of trees and finally got where we needed to be: the portal.

"What do we do now?" asked Xavier, "We're cornered."

"Oh, right," I said. I hadn't exactly thought about that. That was as far as my plan went, and I was surprised

Bailey had not killed us yet. I tried to think of something we could do, and I finally got it. "All right, I know what to do. This guy can control lightning, right?" they all nodded their heads, "So, the only way to beat him is if we get our orbs, then team up and fight him."

"But can't he just hunt us down again?" asked Alex.

"Not if we separate," I said, slyly.

"Great idea!" said Lauren, "But how do we get out of here alive?"

"Hmm," I said, thinking, "I got it! Lauren, sorry, but you'll have to go back to Danville and find a place to stay, probably Eve's house so no one will know you're there, and we'll know where to find you. Xavier, you shoot arrows at Bailey, meanwhile, me, Alex and Roy will charge him."

They all nodded, then Lauren walked into the bush. I turned around to see Bailey about ten feet away from us. He took his sword out of its sheath and walked towards us. His sword had a hilt that looked like mine, but already had an orb in it. It was crackling with electricity, and looked almost blue because of the reflection. I stopped looking at his sword, and charged at him.

I started swinging my sword at him, and Alex and Roy followed my lead. Bailey kept sending electric shocks through us, and I was in serious pain. Then, a light bulb went off in my head.

"He's too strong!" shouted Alex.

"What can we do?" asked Roy.

"Xavier! Distract him by shooting some arrows! Alex, Roy you two try to disarm him while I go get something from the castle!" I said while dodging a bolt of lightning.

"Rick!" shouted Xavier.

"What?"

"Be careful!"

"I will, and you too!"

I ran over to the castle to go get what I wanted. I guess I haven't told you what that was yet. I needed chains, and I was wondering where on earth I would get some. As soon as I got outside the forest, I took a moment to look at the castle.

It used to be beautiful, but after Bailey showed up, the entire place was ruined. The whole castle looked as if it had been abandoned for at least twenty years. The walls were usually gray and majestic, but instead looked black, burnt and worn down. I guess lightning was a more powerful element than I had realized. Just one person had almost destroyed an entire civilization. That was when I thought about the importance of our job. If we didn't defeat Bailey in time, he would completely destroy the wolves, and the foxes would take over the world. I imagined what a world that would be. It was horrible. I saw that the world was completely bare, nothing was alive, and those who were, were starving. It was too much for me to bear, so I stopped imagining. My brain then got back to the real world, and I remembered why I needed to go to the castle in the first place.

I had had enough time to catch my breath, so I started running toward the castle again. I ran past trees and bushes, oddly, no animals. After about five minutes, I got to the castle. I walked inside and went straight to the king's room. I saw more animals in one place than I had ever seen in my life. They were sitting in a very organized fashion. There were all kinds of animals; wolves, bears, raccoons, squirrels, deer, zebras, monkeys, and the list goes on and on. The ceiling was at least twenty feet tall, and was covered in intricate designs and patterns. The walls were black, and the room seemed depressing. I remembered what Kevdak had told us when we had first come into Neosolgis, that the mood of everyone would determine the color of the walls and the mood of the kingdom. I then looked at a few animals and they looked like they were attentively listening to something. I looked to see who or what they were listening to, and I saw that in the king's seat was Kevdak.

At first I was surprised and confused, but it soon made sense. Since Olkin had been captured, there was no one to rule, so it only seemed fit that a very good friend of his would take the throne during the time he was gone. I then actually started listening to what he was saying.

"The foxes have sent their most powerful weapon to destroy us, but we cannot let that bring us down. We are a great and strong nation. We have never failed before, and now is not the time to start! We must strike back! If we are to prevail, we must assemble our forces once more to defeat this boy! Now, who is ready to fight for their kingdom?!" a huge cheering erupted from the crowd and I could barely hear after.

Chapter Seven

I finally walked though the crowd and up to Kevdak. "Ah, Rick, how may I be of your assistance?" he asked.

"I need some chains, do you have any?"

"Of course, but first, can you help me assemble an army? You are very skilled in fighting, am I correct?"

"I guess so, but I'm kind of in a hurry, so-"

He cut me off and said; "No matter, it is a quick job, you will get your chains as soon as we finish."

"Fine," I replied.

"Good, now let's get to work, shall we? All of you, who think they can fight, come with me." More than three fourths of the animals stood up and followed Kevdak. I also followed him, and I still had no idea what I was supposed to be doing. He led everyone out of the room and into another room I didn't even know existed. The door was almost hidden, but if you looked close enough, you could see the outline. It was on the right side of the king's door, after you went through a hallway.

I waited for almost a minute for all of the animals to get in and saw that the room was bigger than the king's room, and there was a reason too. It was the armory. There were metal claws and all sorts of armor hanging on the walls, and in the corner was a forgery. All of the armor was black; apparently the metal was different than in the world I came from.

I then went up to Kevdak and said, "What exactly am I supposed to be doing?"

"You shall be helping animals find the correct weapons for themselves."

"Okay," I said. I walked around, looking for any animals that needed help. First, I found a wolf that just couldn't seem to find the correct size of weapon. The wolf was just like any other one, but looked younger and had a sparkle of excitement in its eye.

"I can't seem to find a claw that's my size." it said in a female voice.

I looked around and found the smallest metal claw, then gave it to the young wolf. She tried it on, and said it fit her perfectly. I did this for many other animals, sometimes finding armor and sometimes weapons. At the end, there was one unusual case. There was a bear that needed a sword. The bear was about six feet tall on its hind legs and had dark brown fur. I never figured out why it wanted a sword, but I got it one. Actually, I made it one. Since there were no swords in the armory, I helped Kevdak make it.

It was a grueling process, and took some work. Kevdak told me to get some leftover broken armor. I searched the entire room and found a broken piece of chest armor hanging on the wall. I brought it over to Kevdak. In the very corner of the room, there was a fireplace made out of bricks with a large bowl sitting in it, Kevdak told me to put the broken armor in the bowl and turn on the fire.

"How exactly do I do that?" I asked.

"Turn the knob on the right side left and right very quickly to create friction." I did what he said, and soon enough, the wood sitting inside was lit on fire. I let the black metal sit in the furnace until it was completely melted. We then took the melted metal and poured it in a large stone that had an indent the shape of a sword's blade. As soon as it got solid, I used a clamp to pick it up and quickly put it in a tub of water that was right next to the rock with a sword shaped indent in it. I then put it back into the rock to cool it down.

The Most Powerful Person in the World Wants to Kill Us

After it was done, Kevdak and I still had to take the blade and attach a hilt. Kevdak went out of the room and came back inside holding a hilt in his mouth. He walked over to me and I took the hilt. It was brown, the exact shade of the bear that needed the sword. It also had a bear on its hind legs as a design on the hilt, and the cross-guard was a dim shade of gold. It was slanting upwards, probably so that something with a bigger hand would be able to use it. I picked up the blade in my other hand, making sure I didn't touch the edges, and put it in the top of the hilt. I had to adjust it a little bit so that the blade would stay in the hilt. When I heard a small clicking sound, I only held the hilt, and the sword was complete. The blade was a light shade of black, and it looked perfect on the golden cross-guard and brown hilt. The sword was also really heavy, but it wasn't for me, so it didn't matter anyways.

I showed it to Kevdak, hoping he would say I was done there, but obviously, I wasn't. He told me that the blade was not sharp enough yet, so I had to sharpen it. I went into the corner and found a table with a large diamond on it. "What is this for?" I asked.

Chapter Seven

"It is the strongest rock that has ever been found, so we use it to sharpen our swords." he answered.

The diamond was completely clear and not worn down at all, even though Kevdak told me it had sharpened over fifty swords. I guessed that was because it would be the sword that got worn down rather than the diamond when scraped together. I put the sword down on the table and held it down with my left hand and picked up the diamond with my right hand. I started scraping the right side of the sword. It made a loud grinding sound, and I tried to do it as fast as I could without damaging the blade. After the sword was completely sharpened on both sides, I had to turn it over and do the same thing. Once that was over, I took the sword back to where Kevdak was standing, right next to the furnace. "A very fine sword," he said, "if I did not know any better, I would think you were a very experienced sword maker."

"That's great and all," I said, "but can you just get me my chains now?"

"Surely," said Kevdak.

"So, where do I get some?" I asked.

"Come with me," he walked through the entire crowd of animals with armor and weapons, and stopped at a bear.

It was the bear that I had made the sword for. The bear took the sword out of Kevdak's mouth and tried it out. "Very nice," it said in a very deep voice, "this is just what I needed. Thank you."

"You're welcome," I said, and with that, I walked out of the room, following Kevdak. As we went outside the room, I took a moment to look at the inside of the castle. The hall seemed to be endless, but that was because it was faded into darkness on the right side. The armory was at the end of the hall, and Kevdak and I were standing in front of the door.

The door was about ten feet tall and had no door handles because it was supposed to be pushed open and would close automatically. It was painted a deep shade of maroon and had golden designs of animals, such as wolves, bears, etc. There were no other rooms in the hall; I guess the wolves never found a reason to make more rooms. The walls were made of bricks, as was the rest of the castle and they were held together by small pieces of black metal. I wondered where you could find that kind of metal, what it was called, and what it was made of.

The bricks were a dark shade of gray, probably because of what Kevdak had explained when Roy, Xavier, Lauren, Alex and I had first gotten to Neosolgis. The interior of the castle was beautiful, but the outside had been completely destroyed.

Right then, Kevdak started walking back the way we came from the king's room. Instead of going inside, Kevdak opened a door that was about fifty feet farther away. I thought it would be a room, but instead, it was a closet. Inside, it was really dark and was not a regular closet, it was in the shape of a U and the tallest shelf was about five feet from the ground.

From one end of the closet to the other, it was about fifteen feet. The shelves had about a foot between each one. The top shelf had the least amount of things on it, and the bottom had the most. I could not tell what most of the objects were, but from what I could see, there were...thinking back on it, I couldn't really tell what anything was.

Since I could only see the outlines of things, everything looked like dark blobs. I saw the figure of Kevdak walk over to the farthest point of the closet and pick something up with mouth from the third shelf. As he turned around and started walking towards me, I saw that he had a long chain in his mouth. I could hear it scraping the floor and hitting itself. Kevdak came up to me and I took the chain from him. "Thanks," I said while walking away.

"Wait!" exclaimed Kevdak, "Why do you feel the need to use chains?"

"You'll find out," I said, acting mysterious. I walked through the hallway and back to the entrance of the castle and went through the hallway on the other side to get to our room. I walked over to the room, turned around and saw that Kevdak wasn't following me anymore. I wondered where he went, but I had more important things to do. I walked into the room and saw four people; Xavier, Alex, Roy, and Bailey. They were each sitting on a bed, except Bailey was lying down on my bed with his eyes closed.

Chapter Seven

"Hey, nice job, you got him. Now, to make sure he doesn't escape, let's put him in the chains I got," I said while dangling the chains in the air.

"I have a question," said Roy, "why can't we just kill him? It would save us a lot of trouble."

"Because," I said, "for one, we are not killers, and two, he might have a lot of useful information."

"Okay, so what do we do with him?"

"That's what I haven't thought about yet," I said, feeling really stupid.

"Let's put him in chains before he becomes conscious again!" shouted Xavier. Realizing that we might not have much time before Bailey woke up; I quickly wrapped the chains around Bailey's whole body, except his head. I tied a knot with the chains around his chest.

After I tied him up, I sat down on Lauren's bed. I guess none of us had anything to say, because for the next few minutes, we were all silent. I was thinking of what we would do with Bailey once he woke up. I was thinking we could ask him a bunch of questions and threaten him. I was also feeling frightened because of the power that one boy had. I was also frightened of myself because once I had found my orb, I might have that kind of power. I found it terrifying that I could, at some point, have someone's life in my hands. I didn't want to have that ability, it would be scary.

When I was about to drift off thinking about something else, I saw Bailey's eyes start to open. Once he was completely awake, I blew my top. "Why were you destroying the castle?!" I screamed.

"Because I had to," he said, calmly.

"You will have to answer our questions or we will never let you go," said Xavier, sounding very serious. At that point, I wondered how Xavier, Alex and Roy had managed to capture such a powerful person, but I didn't have time to dwell on it.

"Okay, but know this: once you let me go, I will show no mercy on you, or the wolves!" said Bailey.

"We know you work with the foxes, so you have to know the location of King Olkin," I said.

"I do not," he said.

"Liar!" shouted Alex while getting up. We kept asking Bailey questions, but we couldn't seem to get him to tell us anything. After five minutes, we ran out of questions to ask, so I just stated something. "Since you won't spill anything, we have no choice but to take you to jail," I said. Right then, Bailey stood up and slipped his arms out of the chains. I hadn't realized how loosely I had tied his chains.

He made a small ball of electricity between his hands and it sank into his chest. His body then became completely charged with electricity. He had bolts of lightning running along every part of body, except his head. As soon as the lightning hit the chains, they exploded. He was out of his chains and my eyes were wide open in shock.

"We have to go get our orbs!" I shouted, "Now!" we each grabbed our maps and weapons and ran out of the castle.

I MEET AN OLD GUY

Rick

I unrolled my map and looked where I would have to go to get to my orb. I had to go north of the castle to find a mountain. I looked back to see if anyone was still behind me, and all I saw was the castle. I looked ahead of me to see if I could make any sense of where I was going, but there was grass as far as the eye could see. There wasn't even a path leading to the mountain! I realized how difficult Eve's dad must have made it to find the orbs, and I thought about what kind of challenges I might have to face.

Chapter Eight

I looked at my map again to see where I had to go, but I honestly had no idea where I was supposed to be headed. I looked to the horizon to see if I was able to see a mountain, but all I could see was the sun.

It was about six o'clock, and the sun was about to set. I had walked for at least an hour or two without knowing it, so I couldn't go back to the castle to for a place to sleep. I guessed I would have to make myself a hut or something. The only problem was that there were no trees for me to build anything on.

I looked to the left and right, but there were no trees in sight. Then, I looked closer, and on the right side was a faint shadow of a tall tree. I decided that it was my only hope, so started running towards it so that I would be able to make it there before the sun set.

I ran as far as I could, but the tree never seemed to get closer, and I couldn't tell how far I had run because the entire area looked the same. I decided to conserve my energy because I might not get anything to eat that night, so I started walking.

As I got closer to the tree, my time started running out; the sun was minutes away from setting. Seeing as I couldn't go back, I kept walking towards the tree. While I was walking, I saw that the outline was becoming a lot bigger.

I walked until sundown, and finally decided that there was no way I would be able to get to the tree with no light, but just then, looked up and saw the moon. It had been my stroke of sheer luck that it had been a full moon that night, so I would be able to get a small amount of light. It wasn't much, but it was enough for me to see. I walked as fast as I could towards the tree, and after about thirty minutes, I got there.

When I arrived, I was amazed at how large that one tree had grown. It was at least two hundred feet tall, but it was probably taller. It had an enormous trunk, it was about fifty feet in diameter, and there were no branches coming out of it until a third of the way up. The branches that did come out of the trunk were about the size of a regular-sized tree's trunk might be. I estimated that the tree had to be at least two to three hundred years old, if it was that size.

One thing I didn't see until a few minutes later was that there was a small cabin made entirely of logs sitting at the base of the tree. I felt even luckier when I saw the cabin because there was a slight chance that whatever lived there would let me stay for the night.

I walked up to the front door and knocked twice. I stood there with a rolled up map in one hand and my sheathed sword on my side, staring at the door, waiting for something to open the door. Finally, the door creaked open, and the weirdest thing opened the door. An old man.

Now, I'm not talking about an animal that looked old and I thought was a guy. No, I'm talking about an actual human man with white and gray hair, a beard, a wrinkled face, and tattered old clothes on.

"Now, how did one as young as you get to a place like this at this time at night?" he asked. At first, I almost couldn't understand him because I had been so used to talking in the animals' language, but this guy had spoken in English.

"Uhh…" I said, very confused and surprised.

"No matter, why don't you come in?"

"Okay," I said, feeling somewhat awkward.

I Meet an Old Guy

I followed him inside his cabin, and it was much bigger than it had looked from the outside. One thing I noticed was that everything was made of wood, and I wondered how long it would have taken to build the place. There were two side-by-side rooms when you walked in and a hallway to the left. There were chairs and couches all made of wood and looked very uncomfortable. We walked into the room on the right side of door. There were couches lined up along the sides and there was a table in the middle.

"Have a seat," he said while making a motion for me to sit down.

I walked over to the wooden chair that was across from the wooden sofa, still in shock from two things. First, was that there was an old *human* man in the world of the *animals*, and second was that he knew English. That meant that he had to have come from my world and somehow gotten here, like how Kevdak had taken us through the portal. I sat down, and felt that the wood was a lot softer than it had looked; it was actually very comfortable.

Chapter Eight

"Now tell me young one," he said while sitting down on the couch, "what are you doing here?"

"I-" I didn't know what to say. *Should I tell him that I came here because I was looking for the orb and I needed a place to stay, or should I make up some lie?* I asked myself.

"I was looking for a treasure that someone told me was far from here, but it got dark outside and I needed a place to stay," I said.

"Then what is that piece of paper you're holding?" he inquired.

"It's a treasure map."

"May I take a look? I might be able to help you; I know this world like no one else."

"No," I quickly responded without thinking. I didn't trust anyone except my friends, because I didn't know that world, and I could never distinguish the difference between the good guys and the bad guys.

"Why not?" he asked, seeming very curious.

"It's a family secret," I lied.

"Okay, I'll respect that," he said, peacefully.

"I still have one request," I said.

"And what would that be?"

"Can I stay here tonight? I promise I'll leave tomorrow morning," I pleaded, hoping that he would say yes.

"All right, stay as long as you need to."

"Thank you sir," I said, "where should I sleep?"

"I'll show you to the guest room," he said while getting up.

I followed him to the hallway, and he led me to a room at the end, and told me that that was my room for the night. I walked inside and all I saw was a bed. That's all there was, the room was about twenty feet wide, and twenty from the entrance to the back wall. I wondered how there was so much room in such a small cabin, but soon realized that the house must have been cutting into the tree's trunk.

I was so tired that I collapsed on the soft, wooden bed as soon as I laid down on it. I went to sleep, and had no idea what I had dreamed about, as usual.

When I woke up the next morning, I was still sleepy and really hungry because I hadn't eaten anything in probably fifteen hours. I got up, started walking, and almost fell over. I walked out of the room to the front where I had come in and saw the old man sitting on the couch.

"Would you happen to have something I can eat?" I asked him, "I haven't eaten in more than twelve hours."

"Sure, come with me," he said.

I followed him outside and he led me around the trunk of the tree and I saw a garden. There were berry bushes of all sorts, and small fruit trees too. "Pick anything that looks good to you, it's all edible."

I looked around and saw some light blue berries on a bush. They looked just like the ones that we had found on Wolf Mountain. I then realized that the berries on Wolf Mountain must have come from Neosolgis. I walked over to the bush because I knew those berries would be safe to eat, and started eating them like I had never eaten before. The bush was about half my height, and there were berries all around it. By the time I was done, I had probably finished about three-fourths the bush. Now, obviously I'm exaggerating a little because, as you know, it's not humanly possible to finish that many berries in one sitting.

I Meet an Old Guy

When I was finished, I was finally not hungry after fifteen hours of no food. I walked out of the garden and to where the old man was standing and said, "I'll be on my way now, thank you for everything, sir."

"Are you forgetting something?" he asked. He looked kind of angry, but like he was trying to hide it.

I wondered what in the world he could possibly be angry about, but I decided to answer him in a pleasant tone, "I think I left my sword next to the bed, now that I think about it," I said.

"I believe you forgot something else as well," he said, now sounding almost frustrated.

I tried to remember what else I had brought with me, and I soon realized that he must have been talking about my map. "Oh, I guess you must be talking about my treasure map," I said, trying to remember what I had called it earlier because I didn't want to contradict myself.

"Indeed," he said.

"I'll just go inside, grab my stuff, and go," I responded.

"Okay."

Chapter Eight

I walked around the enormous tree trunk and into the house/cabin thing. I went through the hallway and into the room I had stayed in the previous night. I saw my sword in its sheath lying on the floor, so I went to pick it up. I picked it up, and hooked it to my belt so I could access it more easily. I walked out of the room, wondering where I had left the map. I went to the outside rooms to check if I had left it there when I had first come in, but it wasn't anywhere to be found.

I searched for probably ten to fifteen minutes, but I couldn't find it anywhere. The old man walked in, and I asked if he had seen my map.

"Yes, in fact I have it here with me," he said. He then pulled a rolled up piece of old parchment from the back pocket of his pants that was hiding under his shirt, so I didn't see it before.

"Thanks," I said while getting up off of the floor and walking towards him, "may I have it back?"

"Not until you tell me where you got this map," he said, now completely serious with a stern expression.

I Meet an Old Guy

"I told you, it's a family secret, I got it from my parents a few years ago," I made up more details to make my lie sound real.

"Lies!" he shouted angrily, "Tell me the truth! Where did you get this map?" each word came out separately, like people do when they're angry and trying to make a statement.

"Wait, how do you know I didn't get this from my family?" I asked suspiciously.

"Because, I looked at it!"

"I thought you said you would respect my privacy!"

"Well, you left the map on the chair, and I wanted to know what it is that you are looking for!" he said, "Where did you get this map?!"

"I-I" I couldn't think of anything else to say, and when I was going to tell him the truth, he cut me off.

"You stole this!"

"No, I didn't! Someone gave it to me!"

"That's impossible! Unless you got it from my daughter," he said.

Chapter Eight

"How would I know your daughter?" I asked, frustrated. Then I realized something, "Wait, did you say your daughter?"

"Yes, what else would I have said?" he asked, definitely angry with me.

"Would your daughter happen to be named Eve Johnson?" I asked.

"So you do know her! I bet you stole this from her!"

"No! I told you, she gave this to me! I'm one of Eve's good friends!"

He stopped, looking confused. I guess we both just found out that the other person wasn't who we thought they were, or something of that sense.

"So, you're Aric Johnson? The Aric Johnson?" I asked in wonder.

"Yes, why?"

"Nobody in the world thinks that you're alive! And I didn't think so either, up until thirty seconds ago. Do you know how mad Eve's going to be when she finds out that you were alive this whole time?"

"I understand. I made a mistake coming here to hide. But it was the only choice I had," he said, finally calming down.

"How did you do it?"

"How did I do what?"

"You know, stay for so long in hiding, and how does nobody know you're here?"

"I will explain everything to you, and then it will all make sense," he said while walking towards the couch, "now, how much of my story do you know?"

"Only that you can control all six elements, you had to hide five of the orbs because the foxes stole one of them, and that one day you mysteriously disappeared and never came back," I said, thinking back to what Corvyre had told us during training.

"All of that is correct, but there was a lot more to it," he said, "you see, it wasn't just me, but I had six friends also. Their names were Valerie, Spencer, Zack, Madison, Sean, and Sarah. We had all the power to control the elements, but I had the special ability to control all six. Valerie could control fire, Spencer could control plants, Zack could control earth, Sean could control water,

Chapter Eight

Madison could control lightning, and Sarah could control air. When we had all graduated from college, the wolves took us here and explained everything to us. By that time, my daughter Eve had recently been born, and I didn't want to leave her. They told us how we could control elements, and how we needed the orbs to become more powerful. They told us about the foxes' kingdom getting larger and stronger, so we needed to defeat them. They gave us the orbs and trained us for years until we were ready to face the foxes.

"We were sent off on a great journey that changed our lives forever. I walked out of the castle with my friends behind me. We had our weapons in our hands, ready to fight. I had a sword, as did three of my friends. The others had bows and arrows. We all had backpacks on that were loaded with supplies for our long trip. We started walking, and it took countless days of nothing but walking to finally get there, and our supplies were running low. It was nightfall, and there was less than a mile to go until we reached their territory. We slept on the ground, and when we woke up, there was an army of foxes waiting for us.

I Meet an Old Guy

"We went into battle unprepared, and they foxes probably had decent rest and were ready to fight. I had no idea how they could have known we were coming, but thinking back on it, the only way was if someone had told them. I suspect that there is a traitor in the wolf kingdom. Anyway, we charged into battle with our weapons in our hands and were getting powered by the orbs. I shot some lightning at the foxes and killed a few of them. I hate the idea of taking a life, but it was the only way to survive, otherwise I wouldn't be here right now. I ran forward, shooting lightning in random directions, trying not to get myself killed. Meanwhile, Valerie created columns of fire shooting up from the ground, burning the foxes, and sometime badly injuring them. Sean summoned an entire pond from somewhere nearby to be under his control. He shot bits of water at hundreds of miles per hour at any fox who tried to attack him while holding the entire pond above his head. Zack created a wall of earth around the foxes, except in the front so they couldn't escape, but we could still attack them. Spencer made plants grow vigorously and start to strangle some foxes, or just hold them in place like sitting ducks. Madison created a huge ball of electricity and shot giant bolts of lightning out of it. Sarah was shooting streams of air from her palms at the foxes, blowing them back at the wall of earth. I then took a chunk of earth out of the ground and flung it forwards. We were all controlling elements side-by-side and using them to try and defeat the foxes, but I soon saw that there were too many of them for us to handle without getting tired. Realizing this, I devised a plan for us to defeat them all with one single move. It involved using all the elements at once, and since I didn't have the energy to do it all by myself and I couldn't control more than one element at a time, I needed everyone's help. I closed the wall of earth, completely trapping all of the foxes in. Right before my friends were going to send their next attack, they stopped, looking at me in confusion.

'Why'd you do that?' asked Zack.

'I have a plan, and it involves all of us,' I said while signaling for all of them to come closer.

'What's your plan?' asked Madison.

'First, Sarah and I need to make a tornado, and then I need I need Sean to get some water in it to turn it into a hurricane, next Madison adds some lightning around it, and Spencer, you need to tie all of the foxes down with plants so that they are immobile,' I said

'Well what about me?' asked Zack.

'When the time comes, I need you to create an opening in the wall so that the hurricane can get inside. Then, once the wall is opened, Valerie needs to set the plants on fire, so that the foxes will burn. '

'All right,' he said.

'Let's go!' I shouted.

"Sarah and I started swirling air in a circle in unison, but it was very difficult, and I had never done it before. The air got easier to move as we got it going, but the tricky part was making it big enough.

'You do the bottom and I'll do the top!' I shouted.

"She nodded her head in approval as I stopped swirling the air near the ground and started swirling it directly above where I had been before. It was a lot harder that time because I was doing it by myself. I spun the air around as fast as I could, and soon enough, it connected with the bottom and started looking like a tornado because it was collecting dust and looked gray.

Chapter Eight

"Sean had been ready with the water floating above him, so when I told him to put it in, it got dumped in right away. Sean actually had some more work to do though. He had to keep the water around the tornado to keep it from fling away. The water spread out around the entire tornado, so it looked more like a hurricane.

"We moved the hurricane closer to the wall Zack had created, and I told Spencer to hold down the foxes with plants. Once he said he was done, we moved the hurricane closer to the wall, and seeing that, Zack opened up the front of the wall again, leaving enough room for the hurricane to slip inside. When it opened, I saw the foxes being held in place because plants had grew on top of them. We then let the hurricane loose on the foxes. Valerie then created a fire on some plants, and soon enough, the fire spread to all the foxes. When the hurricane got close enough, it tore the foxes from the ground and they started swirling around in the air. After a little while, there were no foxes left on the ground. The only thing left to do was to stop the hurricane.

'Stop the hurricane!' I yelled as loud as I possibly could to everyone else.

I Meet an Old Guy

Apparently they heard me because Sean took all of the water out of the mix, and Sarah stopped controlling the air, and Madison stopped shooting lightning. Then, just as I had suspected, all of the foxes went flying in different directions, and most of them hit the wall.

'I guess our work here is done,' said Sean, while putting the water back where it belonged.

'What do we do now?' asked Valerie.

'Well, I think our only choice is to go back to the castle,' said Spencer, 'unless someone has a better idea.'

"We all shook our heads, and with that, we started our journey back to the castle. The battle had taken up a few hours, so we were all really tired, but we kept going anyways. On the way back to the castle, nothing exciting happened, but it took a few days to walk back."

"Is that all?" I asked.

"No, there is more, but I will warn you, it's not as happy as the first part of the story," said Aric.

"That's okay," I said, "I want to know what really happened."

Chapter Eight

"All right," he said, "here we go again. When we finally got back to the castle, it was almost nightfall. We went inside the front and to our rooms."

"Wait, you had your own rooms?" I asked, "We have to share one! That's not fair!"

"Life is not always fair." Aric said, "When I got into my room, I immediately collapsed on my bed. The others had to secure their orbs in a safe place, so that no one could find them, but I had the luxury of falling asleep right away, seeing as I didn't have an orb.

"I was woken up a few hours after I went to sleep by loud noises coming from inside the castle itself. I walked outside, trying to find out what exactly was going on, when Corvyre-"

"You knew Corvyre?" I asked.

"Yes, we all did," he answered," Now will you let me finish my story without getting interrupted?"

"Sorry," I said. I could feel my face turning red; I hate it when people tell me stuff.

"When Corvyre came up to me, she said, 'We have been attacked by the foxes, and they have come looking for the orbs, they found one already, you are our last hope. Go find the others and hide them so that the foxes cannot find them!'

"I ran to my friends' rooms as fast as I could; and because I knew where they had hidden their orbs, my job became easier. I ran in an out of each of their rooms, taking their orbs and putting them in my backpack. It seemed as though they were all still sleeping, and none of them would wake up, no matter how much noise I made. Then, I figured out what had happened. They were all dead; they had been ambushed, murdered in their sleep."

I could see Aric's eyes tearing up, and I could hear his voice shaking as he was talking. I couldn't even imagine the pain of losing my six best friends, and on top of that, having to tell a story about it to someone? I couldn't stay quiet any longer, so I started talking. "If you don't want to, you don't have to talk about anymore," I said.

"No," said Aric, "you need to know what truly happened.

"I screamed in shock from what had just happened, and I soon burst out in tears, but I knew I had to keep going. When I ran outside of the castle, I got attacked by foxes. My fear soon turned into rage, and I was blinded by what they had done to my friends, and I was out for revenge. I blasted the foxes with lightning that shot out of my fingertips, I strangled some with plants, others I set on fire or crushed them between rocks. I did anything I could to avoid getting hurt, and did everything I could to make sure the foxes did.

"I ran away from the castle, and once I was back to my senses, I thought of places to hide the orbs. I took maybe a week or two hiding the orbs, and I made my own paper using the elements. I grew a small tree and cut it by slicing it with the air. I then created a large mortar and pestle out of earth. I put part of the tree in the pestle and started smashing it with the mortar. I then remembered that I needed water, so I found an underground river and pulled some water out. I put it in the pestle with the crushed tree trunk and turned it into a paste. Next, I created a table of earth with a very small indent the shape of a rectangle. I poured the paste in, and let it sit. To make it dry faster, I blew it with air. When it was finally dried, there was one last thing I had to do. I cut some more of the tree and used the logs as firewood. I started a fire, and held the dried paste over it to make it crisp. Once I had done that, I had to repeat the same process four more times. After a few hours, I had my own sheets of brown paper to draw maps on. Luckily, I had brought a pencil in my backpack, and I used it to draw. I had finished just before nightfall, so I rolled up the maps, put them in my backpack, lied down, and went to sleep. When I woke up, I ate some berries that I had grown myself, and took off towards the castle. It took a few days to get back, and I was surprised to see that the castle was still there because the foxes had invaded."

"I was met by Corvyre at the front door, and she had something to tell me. 'Aric, you cannot stay here any longer; the foxes will come and hunt you down because of what you and your friends had done to their army,'

'I have to go to my family anyways,' I said.

'Then you must not come back to this world, unless you wish to die,' said Corvyre.

"I set off for the portal, to go back to the world I came from. When I reached the portal, I turned around to get one last look at Neosolgis, and then I went through. When I got to the other side, I went back to my family. Eve was merely one year old at the time, and she was a very noisy little girl. She learned to talk when she was about nine months old; she was amazing. The first thing I heard when I got home was, 'Daddy! Where did you go? Was it fun? Did you bring me anything?'

'I did bring you something,' I said. I pulled the maps out of my backpack and handed them to Eve to look at.

'What are these?' she asked.

'They're maps, and I need you to do me a huge favor,' I said.

'What? What do you want me to do?' she asked eagerly.

'I will put these in a safe place, and you must never give these to anyone, unless you are sure that they are in desperate need of them,' I said quietly.

'Okay!' she whispered. I then went into her room with the maps, and came back without them. 'They are in a safe place now!' Eve exclaimed.

"That night, I realized how much explaining I would have to do to everyone in that world because I had gone away with six friends, but I was the only one that came back alive. They would have thought I killed all of them, so I ran away. I came here in secret from the wolves and have been living here ever since. I grew many trees, only to cut them for wood to make my house from."

"So you left your family twelve years ago and they think you're dead? Do you know how mad Eve will be when she finds out that you're still alive and that you were here the whole time?" I asked.

"I know, but I thought this was the best thing to do, and I can't turn back now," said Aric.

"Running away from your problems is not the way to solve them," I said. It felt weird giving someone older than me advice. Usually it would be the other way around.

"Well what can I do about it now?" he asked.

"You can go back there and apologize to your family. I've already brought Eve to this world, so you can explain everything to her," I said.

"You did what?!" he exclaimed.

"I brought Eve here," I said somewhat slowly, confused at why Aric was mad.

"Why would you bring someone who cannot control an element here?! She doesn't belong in Neosolgis, that's why I had kept it a secret from my family! Sooner or later, she will tell one of her friends about this place, and the news will somehow reach everyone on the face of the earth in a matter of days! After that they will all want to come to this world, looking for more open land, and there will be no way to stop them! Do you understand the implications of what you have done?!" he screamed.

Well, I thought to myself, *that just took an unexpected turn for the worse.*

"What was I supposed to do to convince her to give me the map?" I asked

"Anything but bringing her here!" Aric yelled.

"Well there's no point in arguing over it now!" I said, "It already happened, there's no way we can change it!"

"You're right," he said, "but don't you have something to find?"

I had completely forgotten about finding my orb because I had been so caught up in Aric's story, and arguing with him. "Well, thanks for everything," I said, "I'll be on my way."

"Do you need any food or supplies of any kind?" he asked.

"Some food and water would be nice," I said.

I Meet an Old Guy

"I'll be right back," he said. Aric got up, went outside for a few minutes, and came back with a small basket full of all different kinds of berries and a jar full of water. "Here you go," he said while handing me the stuff.

"Do you have a backpack or something?" I asked.

"Ah, I can give you the one that I always used to use," he said. He walked in the hallway, and when he came out, he was holding a regular sized, green backpack that had pockets everywhere. "Make sure you give this back to me."

"I sure will," I said, smiling.

I put the food and water in the backpack, slung it on my shoulders, and left.

PROBLEMS WITH THE MOUNTAIN'S PEAK

Rick

I walked outside with my sword at my side, my map in my backpack and the hope of accomplishing something in my head. I took the map out of my backpack to see where I needed to go next. I needed to keep going south of the castle, and I guessed it would be straightforward from there. I kept walking until I got hungry, and every so often I would eat some berries or drink some water.

There was nothing exciting happening on my walk, so I'm not going to make you sit through me going on and on about how tired I was, or how there was nothing to do, or how it was burning hot outside. I'm going to skip all the boring stuff and get right to the exciting part.

I looked around, and all I could see were a few mountains in distance. Around me, there were bushes and seemingly endless grassland. The grass would move with the wind, making almost no noise. My footsteps were the loudest thing to be heard, along with the backpack bumping against my back as I walked. It was close to sundown, and I could still see everything around me.

I sat down to take a short rest, when I heard a faint rustling sound coming from a bush nearby. At first I thought it was just the wind, until I heard it again. This seemed all too familiar, it had happened to me before, when the wolves were trying to get my attention. I got up, wondering what animal would be calling to me this time.

When I got to the bush, I saw a fox, curled up in its sleep, its tail flicking the delicate branches of the small bush. I knew that was a bad sign. The foxes were evil, and I wondered if it was a coincidence, or if it had been following me. I didn't want to take a chance to find out. I walked away slowly, trying not to make any noise. I started walking in the same direction I had been going in the first place as fast as I could without making much sound. I kept on walking for a while, until I tripped on a rock I couldn't see, and fell. I hoped that the fall hadn't been loud enough for the fox to hear.

I was completely wrong. I heard the fox get up and start running towards me. I wasn't sure I would have to fight it, so I took my backpack off just in case I had to. It ran up in front of me, and stopped. It looked like it was getting ready to attack me, so I took my sword out of its sheath. I got in my fighting stance, just like Corvyre had taught me, and the fox jumped at me.

I didn't know what to do because I didn't want to kill it, and I didn't want to get killed either. I simply moved out of the way and let the fox hit the ground. I kept my sword pointed at it, like as if I was threatening it. It jumped at me again, but this time, I slashed my sword, cutting its leg in midair. It fell to the ground with only three legs to stand on, and it could barely stand.

"I'll spare your life if you give me all the information I need," I said, with my sword and inch away from the fox's neck.

"Okay," it whimpered.

"First, tell me who sent you here," I said in a demanding tone.

"It was the human, the one with the power to control lightning," it said, still sounding scared.

"Bailey," I whispered, "Now, do you know the location of King Olkin?"

"N-no, sir," it said.

"Don't lie to me," I said.

"I'm not l-lying," said the fox.

"Yes you are!" I shouted, "Now tell me where he is!" I pushed my sword to its neck, so that it I added the slightest bit of pressure, it would cut its throat open.

"Okay, if you go into our castle, go all the way to the end of the hall. There should be a long, spiraling staircase that leads to the dungeon. When you get there, you will see cells lined up on both sides, and Olkin should be in the seventh one on the left side," it said, unwillingly.

"You have been of much help to me, so I will spare your life," I said. I sheathed my sword, turned around and picked up my backpack. I kept walking towards the mountain, and it was minutes from sundown. I decided to lie down and get some rest because I would need it for the following day.

I lied down on the soft grass, using the backpack as a pillow. I slept peacefully that night, under the bright moon, with the gentle wind blowing my hair, and the sound of crickets chirping slowly putting me to sleep.

I woke up the next morning, not knowing whether I was sleepy, or hungry. I had a little bit of food and water left, so I tried to ration it. I had a few pounds of berries and water. I got up, rubbed my eyes, and tried to calculate how long it would take me to get to the mountain. I figured that it might take half a day's journey.

I had no time to lose, so I started walking right away. It was a little past midday when I got there, and it was maybe eighty or ninety degrees outside. I stopped for a small lunch, and took an hour break. What I would have given for some real food, like a burrito or something. I had been living off of only fruits and vegetables for the past week or so. Just thinking about it made me want some even more.

I finished my break, and I looked up. The mountain was colossal. It was probably two or three times taller than Wolf Mountain, and it was definitely a whole lot steeper. There were trees, bushes, and plants of all kinds growing on it. That was one sight you didn't see in the world I come from. Humans had destroyed almost all of nature, and they didn't try to do anything about it. Well, people recycle and stuff, but when was the last time someone actually did something about the environment? That was one thing I loved about the world I was in; nature was untouched, and everything lived in harmony with it, rather than destroying it for your own luxury. Now, I'm not saying that I'm not guilty of these thing too, don't get me wrong, I am simply stating the problems with the way we humans live.

Anyways, I would run into some serious problems if I tried to get to the top in one go. I noticed that at the very top, it was snowing heavily in the middle of summer. Don't ask me how that works, because to this day, I still have no idea.

It looked almost as if there was a blizzard at the top, and I knew I couldn't survive that kind of weather in shorts and a t-shirt. Even if I could, I would have no chance of getting to the peak without getting piled in snow.

I guess my only choice is to go back to the castle, wait for the others, and admit to them that I couldn't get my orb, I thought.

I turned around, running short on food and water, and headed back to the castle. It was a long and agonizing trip back because I had little water and it was burning hot outside. At the end of the day, I was almost there, maybe half an hour's walk away.

A PASSAGE

Alex

I ran out of the castle with everyone else. I had my sword in its sheath on my side and the map in my hand. I had never bothered to look at the map before, so I had no idea where I should be going.

I ran in the direction that no one else ran in, and when I got far enough, I unrolled the map to see where I was actually supposed to go. I looked at it, and there was no map at all. It was a piece of paper with a riddle written on it in big letters. Lucky for me, it was written in English. It read: *Hot or cold when nations unite, those five circles are their might, yet without this flame there shall be no game.*

What the heck could that mean? I wondered. *Without this flame there shall be no game.* I loved playing games, especially sports. My dad had hired coaches for all kinds of sports like soccer, basketball, tennis, football, baseball, and badminton. I didn't like badminton as much, but it was still pretty fun. The question was, what kinds of games could animals play? They obviously couldn't play baseball, basketball, football, or badminton.

I imagined some wolves in basketball jerseys, standing on their hind legs dribbling a ball up and down a court. It was an odd thought. *They might just be able to play a game like soccer though,* I thought, *but does Neosolgis have nations? And would they ever unite?* When I thought of nations uniting and soccer, I immediately thought of FIFA. I had gone to FIFA in 2006, but I barely remember what happened because I was so small, I just remember it being a lot of fun.

I soon remembered that there was a maniac guy after me that wanted to kill me. I didn't exactly have anywhere to go, seeing as my so-called map had turned out to be a piece of paper with a riddle on it. I only had one place I could go, and that was back to the castle. I ran back, but there were lots of foxes everywhere, aimlessly scratching at the walls. I didn't understand what that would do, because the castle was probably made of cement or something of the sort. I went around the side of the castle with no foxes, and sneaked inside.

I went into our room and sat down on my bed. I looked at the riddle one more time, and I still had no idea what it could be talking about. *Why am I the one stuck with the riddle? I'm no good at solving problems! Lauren's the genius, why couldn't she have been the one that got the riddle? I bet Roy, Xavier and Rick are out having the greatest adventure of their lives, while I'm stuck here with a stupid riddle that doesn't make any sense.*

I waited in my room for a few hours, with nothing to do except think about the stupid riddle. It was the most boring time of my life. I got so tired of waiting for the other guys, but what could I have done? If I walked outside, Bailey would be there, waiting to kill me.

Chapter Ten

So, I can't go outside, unless I want to get killed, but if I stay in here too long, the foxes might take over and kill me anyways. I was stuck between a rock and a hard place. It seemed like there was no way to get out of that situation alive. I thought back to when I was learning about how castles were built in my history class the year before, and I had luckily been paying attention. "Every castle has a dungeon, and every dungeon has a passage," my history teacher had said.

That's it! I thought, *The only way out would be through a secret passageway in the dungeon!*

I got up, while wondering whether the castle even had a dungeon in the first place. According to my history teach, it would, and since teachers are "always right!", I decided to search for a dungeon. Obviously, that wasn't the actual reason I was looking for a dungeon, it was because that was the only way I would survive.

I walked out of the room, and to the hallway that led to the king's room. It had huge doors that were painted a shade of maroon and were lined with gold. I kept walking until the end of the hallway, and there were only two more rooms. I had gone inside the first one, and it was a closet. The second door was the armory. There were no secret passageways either.

I got to the end of the hallway, and shouted, "Why is there nothing here?!" I stomped my foot on the ground, and it made a hollow sound. I did it again, and the same thing happened. I looked closely at the ground, and I saw that the square I was standing on was made of wood, and the rest was made of bricks. I lifted the wood, and instead of leading to a large set of stairs, there was a small sloping patch of ground that led down.

I went down, and it led to a dungeon. It had jail cells on both sides, and at the end was a regular-sized door. I ran past the cells, and to the door. I opened the door, and it led to yet another hallway.

Another hallway, are you kidding me?

I went through it anyways. It was pitch-black inside, so I ran into the wall a few times. After that, I created a small fire in the palm of my right hand so that I could see a few feet in front of me. It seemed to go on for almost a mile, and I was bored and tired. At one point, I could hear the faint roaring of animals battling above me. I got to the end of the tunnel, and there was a staircase leading up.

Chapter Ten

Who designed this place, and why did they make it so far away until you can get out?

I walked up the staircase, and at the top was a giant boulder. I tried to move it with my left hand, but I wasn't strong enough. I put out the small fire so I would be able to move the rock. I pushed as hard as I could, but I only moved a few inches. I carefully went down the stairs, and ran back up so I would have more force.

I pushed the rock enough so that I could barely slip out. I walked out, and I noticed that I was near the portal again. I had stepped out into the forest. Well, what used to be a forest. It was all burnt, and there was not a single tree standing that was still alive. I sat down on the closest tree stump, and waited there.

QUAKES IN THE CAVE

Roy

I followed the others outside, not exactly sure what I should be doing. I saw everyone looking at their maps and running in different directions, so I did the same thing. I looked at my map, and it said that my orb was in a cave under a mountain north of the castle. I ran in the direction that it looked like my orb was in, and it seemed like a really long walk.

I hate walking to faraway places. Why couldn't Eve's dad have hidden them somewhere close to the castle, or even in the castle, that way, we wouldn't have to go anywhere. But then again, anyone could find them, and it would have been pointless to hide them.

I was being lazy, like always.

I just defeated the most powerful dude in the world, so don't I deserve a break? I didn't want any of this to happen to me in the first place; I never believed it, until we got here.

I finally got over it, and I started walking. I always complain about things, but I never do anything about it. I walked aimlessly for a few hours, and I got more tired than I had ever been. I had probably walked at least ten miles from the castle; more than I thought I would ever walk at one time in my life.

I sat down, with nothing to do but look at the view. The problem: there was nothing to see. In front of me, I could see some tiny mountains in the distance, and to my left was the faint shadow of a huge tree. The sun was about to set, and I had nowhere to go. Even if I did, it would probably be really far from there, so I wouldn't go anyways.

I just got up and kept walking so I wouldn't have to as much the next day. It was finally dark enough for me to go to sleep, but I had nothing to sleep on and there were so many annoying bugs around.

I lied down on the soft grass, and it wasn't as bad as I had thought. I put my hands under my head, turned to the side and tried to sleep. At first, I couldn't sleep because of all the bugs, but when I started to ignore them, I heard crickets chirping, and the sound was hypnotizing. I fell asleep, and I don't exactly remember my dream.

It's always hard to remember a dream when you wake up, unless it's something so weird that you can't help but remember it. Dreams seem so real while you're dreaming, and you can never tell if it's real or not, but when you wake up, it seems totally unrealistic. I wonder why that is.

Anyway, (sorry, I sometimes drift into random thoughts when I'm thinking, but don't worry, you'll get used to it) I woke up wanting to go back to sleep, like all people would. If you don't, you're...let's leave it at special. I got up because I knew I had to go find my orb, and if I didn't, Bailey might destroy the world, and obviously nobody wants that to happen (hopefully...).

Chapter Eleven

I kept walking toward the mountains in the distance, and I couldn't get over the fact that I still hadn't given up yet. I looked at my map again; just to be sure I wasn't going in the wrong direction, like I usually would be. I opened it up and it seemed like I was going in the right direction, so I stuck with it.

I walked for hours, and I was more tired than I had ever been in my life. One time, I had been running the mile for school, and I sprinted the entire way, so I got around seven minutes, and after that, I was dead. I could barely breathe, but after walking for a few hours toward the mountains, I felt like passing out. I found some corn plants near the mountain, and it was the first meal I had in more than twelve hours. It didn't even cross my mind that they could be poisonous, but luckily, I didn't die. I never thought I would be able to survive on that little food, but I guess I did it. I grabbed the corn, and ate as much as I could so I wouldn't get that hungry again. It was kind of hard to eat, but it was food, and it was sweet.

I got to the mountain, and it was really loud. The mountain my map had been pointing to was a tall one; luckily I didn't have to climb it. Around me, there were only grass and trees and bushes. I walked to the side to see if there was any cave, like my map said.

I found a cave, but I would have died if I went inside. The ground inside was shaking and there were cracks in the ground a few feet wide and about ten feet long. The cave seemed to go on in all directions forever, but that was because I could barely see anything.

How am I supposed to find my orb in here? I would die if I even stepped inside! Was Aric going to try to kill anyone who comes here? I can't do this! I guess my only choice is to go back to the castle.

I turned around, and started walk back to where I came from.

THE LAKE

Xavier

I slung my quiver over my shoulder; picked up my bow in one hand and my map in the other, and ran outside from Bailey, who seemed like he wanted to kill us. And obviously, we *all* wanted to die, right? If you're thinking *right*, then you probably don't like me or any of my friends. Anyways, I had already looked at and memorized my map so I wouldn't waste time when I actually have to find my orb. I like to think ahead.

The weird thing was that rolled up in my map, was a small ring, but I had no idea whose it was. I didn't tell anyone about it, and I definitely didn't give it back to

The Lake

Eve. I kept it in my pocket the whole time, because I knew that anything you find might come in handy later in your life. You never know what might happen.

My map had said that the orb would be in a lake west of the castle, so I ran westward. I had to run through a forest, and then I got really tired and stared walking. I had picked up some vegetables on the way, so I wouldn't starve later. Once again, thinking ahead.

I had walked out of the forest while eating small portions of my food, saving the rest for later. I was expecting the lake to be somewhere near the castle, because that's what Aric made it look like on the map. But it wasn't like that at all. Once I got out of the forest, which had gone on for miles, there wasn't a lake in sight.

I was going to turn around; because there was no way I would be able to find a lake out there, but if there was one thing I had learned, it was to never give up. You want to know why? I bet you do, (because we *all* love hearing Xavier tell life lessons.) Even if you don't want to hear it, too bad, I'm going to tell you, because nothing exciting happened to me for a while anyways.

Chapter Twelve

I was about ten years old, and it was the national math competition (yes, I'm a nerd, but don't mention it again). I was in the top five people, and I had five problems left. The first three people to finish would advance to the final three, and the winner of that would, well, win; obviously. I got to the final three, and the problems just kept getting harder. I was on the last problem, and I couldn't seem to figure it out. I checked my answer a couple times, but it didn't work. I finally gave up, and accepted that I had lost. The guy who won first place got really famous and got all the glory, but I was forgotten. After that, I learned never to accept defeat, and always keep going, no matter how hard it might seem.

After a few hours of walking, I had almost run out of vegetables, and I wasn't hungry at all. It was almost sunset, and I still hadn't found a lake. I kept walking until about forty minutes after sunset, but I actually had no idea how long it had been because I had no clock. I laid down with my bow and what food I had next to me, and I used my quiver (without any arrows in it) as a pillow. It was made of a material similar to leather, so I was kind of comfortable.

The Lake

When I woke up, I ate what was left of my stock of food. It wasn't much, but at least I would survive. I put my arrows back in the quiver and slung it over my shoulder. I picked up my bow that was lying next to me, and started to walk, yet again.

I walked until it was maybe about noon (I figured that much because the sun was right above me), and I could finally see a lake. The vegetables I had eaten had some water in them, but I hadn't had any actual water in a long time. I sprinted for as long as I could so that I would get water faster.

I finally reached the shore, and I started drinking the water immediately. It was more refreshing than you would ever believe. Even though it was a little dirtier than purified water that we were all used to, at least it wasn't the ocean (I can't even imagine drinking ocean water).

I spent the next hour or so looking for food, and I found some apple and orange trees growing near there, so I snacked on those. After that, I started to look for my orb. I figured that it would be somewhere near the center of the lake, because that's what it showed on the map.

Chapter Twelve

I can definitely get to the center of a lake without drowning, I thought, while rolling my eyes, *was Aric trying to kill anyone who tries to get this orb? The guy made a map, so he should have at least made it accessible.*

I tried pushing the water with all my might so I would be able to walk to the center and get it. I was barely able to keep the water off of the shore. Corvyre was right; I could barely do anything with the element before I got the orb. After a while, I gave up, because there was nothing I could do about it.

I sat on a rock that was on the shore, took my shoes off, and let the water run over my feet as the tide was pushed and pulled. My quiver and bow were sitting next to me, and I sat there until I heard some unnatural sounds coming from the lake.

I jumped off the rock, dried my feet off, put on my shoes and readied my weapon. I stepped a few feet back from the shore and pointed my bow and arrow at the sound of the noise. It had gotten kind of dark outside, so I obviously couldn't see as well as I had been able to before.

The Lake

The noise got louder, and I could tell that it was the sound of something swimming towards me, and it wasn't just one thing. I saw five or six figures walk out of the water, and they were walking right towards me. They were long, but barley a foot and a half off the ground, so it led me to one conclusion. I was about to be attacked by crocodiles.

Crocodiles, seriously? I thought, *my life has the weirdest sense of humor.*

They made a hissing noise as they approached me, and it seemed like they were mad. I didn't want to hurt them, but I was more concerned about them attacking me.

"I do not want to fight you," I said in the language of the animals.

They didn't stop attacking, they only came closer. I pulled the string on my bow back, and let the arrow loose on a crocodile. For those of you who have never used a bow before, it's harder than it looks. You have to aim an arrow, and at the same time pull back a string with about fifteen to twenty pounds of pressure.

The arrow hit the crocodile square in the back and probably killed it. I didn't want to have to fight them, but if I didn't, I would die instead. They started surrounding me, and trying to bite me or scratch me. One of them scratched my leg, and it stung like anything. I had shot all of my arrows, and I had only killed two of them. The rest of them surrounded me, and I had no choice but to give up.

I put my hands in the air like I was surrendering and said, "You defeated me, now what, you're going to take me to your leader?"

"Yes," it hissed in a creepy way.

"Oh, I was joking about that, but OK," I said.

One of the crocodiles turned around, and whipped the back of my knees so I would fall down. Another one took my quiver off my back and shoved it over my head so I wouldn't be able to see. I thought ahead, like I always do, and decided not to resist or else they might do something worse. They put me on two of their backs and walked somewhere. I obviously couldn't tell where they were taking me, since I had a freaking arrow holder over my head.

A quiver, really? These guys really don't know how to kidnap someone. I'm just making it easier for them.

The Lake

I was very uncomfortable because crocodiles have pointy backs. Suddenly they started swimming, and then they plunged in the water. I was taken completely by surprise, so I started flailing. The crocodiles each held one of my arms and pulled me down with them. I barely had any air left because I hadn't known that I would get pulled under water. Finally, they pulled me into a cave that was only halfway filled with water.

I immediately floated to the top, and took a huge breath of air. The crocodiles were still pulling me along by my arms, and they had very rough skin. I could also hear a few more crocodiles swimming ahead of the ones that were pulling me.

"Why did we not kill this creature?" I heard one whisper to another.

"Because, I have never seen anything like this, and it can speak our language, so I think the king should decide what to do with it."

They stopped swimming and told me to take the quiver off my head and start walking. I took the quiver off my head, and I saw that there was suddenly no more water. It was somehow lighted, and I looked around to see that there were some crystals giving off light. The next thing I noticed was that I was in a cave.

A cave, really? Where the heck are these things taking me? Well, I shouldn't complain, maybe they'll lead me to my orb. Everyone loves a free passage.

I followed the crocodiles for a while, and suddenly there was a huge room with many passageways. Probably only one of them led to the right place, anyone that knows how underground passages work would have known that.

There were about ten to twelve different ways, and I followed the four crocodiles into the one to the left. After walking for a while, there was a room with one giant crocodile standing in the back. It was the biggest crocodile I would ever see. Now, when I say big, I don't just mean big, I mean huge. It was about three feet off the ground, about seven to ten feet long and looked old. The guy was a dark shade of green, and looked wrinkly.

I figured that the guy must be the king that they had been talking about earlier, obviously. Almost anyone would have figured that out.

The Lake

"Sir," said the crocodile in the front, "we found this creature, we don't know what it is, but it tried to attack us and it can speak our language. We decided to let you determine what to do with it."

"I have seen a creature like this once before, you were too small to remember, but he was a good friend of mine. I believe they are called *humans*. My friend had given me something very important, and told me to only give it to another one of his kind that speaks our language and has an artifact that matches the one I have," the king spoke slowly, in a deep voice, and walked towards me.

"What did your friend give you? And what was your friend's name that gave this thing to you?"

"His name was Aric, and he told me the human who had a *ring*, as he called it would be the one I would give this orb to."

"I have a ring," I said while reaching into my drenched shorts pocket. I pulled out the small ring that had come rolled up inside my map and showed it to the old king.

He pushed something forward from under his hand, and I picked it up. It was a ring identical to the one I had.

Chapter Twelve

"I never thought this day would come," said the king, "follow me, I have something to give you."

I followed him to the back of the room and he showed me an orb. It was a bit bigger than the size of my fist, and it looked awesome, like I had expected. It had a jagged, scaly pattern surrounding it and the scales looked rough. Some of them were dark blue, some were light blue, and others were a light shade of lavender.

I took the orb out of the old king's hand, and as soon as I touched it, I felt powerful. More powerful than I had ever felt in my entire life. "Thank you," I said, "I will be on my way."

"You are very welcome," said the old king.

I had no need for someone to guide me back to the lake because I had already memorized where the crocodiles had led me so I would be able to get out on my own, in case it was a trap. Thinking ahead always pays off.

I walked all the way back to where the cave was half filled with water again, and since I had my orb, I decided to try it out. I had my quiver slung over my shoulder and the orb in one hand. I went near the water, and did the same thing I did when I was first learning to control water; listen to it, and touch it, but it took a lot less time to be able to only hear the water. I think the orb was already working.

I moved my hands outwards and the water parted to the sides of the cave. "Sweet," I whispered to myself. Corvyre had actually been right; I could do much more with the water orb. I walked all the way to the end of the cave and got surrounded by water, but that would never be a problem for me again. I used the water to propel myself to the surface, and I got there in a matter of seconds.

I swam to the shore, walked out to where I had left my bow, and I picked it up. I had my quiver over my shoulder, my orb in one hand, and my bow in the other. Then, I remembered something else Corvyre had said about the orbs.

After you get your orb and it is placed into your weapon, something different will happen to each of your weapons depending on the element of the orb.

Chapter Twelve

I took my orb and put it in the spot in my bow that was perfectly fit for the orb. When I placed it inside, nothing happened.

Was Corvyre lying, or did she just not know what she was saying? Oh well, at least I got the orb, and that's what counts.

I took a last drink of water, turned around, and headed back to the castle.

THE CONQUERING

Bailey

The army of wolves was standing in front of their castle, just as I had known they would do. The army wasn't entirely made up of wolves though. There were other animals too, like deer, monkeys, bears, and many others.

I told the foxes not to take a break, I knew this would happen. Those insolent little animals, what were they thinking, not listening to me, trying to convince me to let them go. It's entirely their fault if we lose the battle, but that would never happen, the wolves are too weak.

Chapter Thirteen

"Charge!" I yelled to my army. I ran to the other army, and stood in front of them for a few seconds. Then, I kept charging at them, and my army followed. I shot some random bolts of lightning at the other side. The foxes jumped and attacked every animal they could. The wolves and other animals were clearly outnumbered, and clearly outmatched, there was no way that we could possibly lose. Even though the other side had fancier weapons, the foxes obviously had more skill and training.

After a few minutes, I decided to jump in, so the battle would get over faster. I walked to the battlefield and started shooting lightning at animals. The battlefield was directly in front of the entrance to the castle. I shot lightning at animals that were somewhat strong, so it would make it a lot easier for my army to defeat them.

From my side, I saw a bear charging at me on its hind legs. In its front paws, it was holding a sword. It had dark brown fur, and it was about six feet tall. I quickly took out my sword charged with lightning, and blocked its first strike. If there was one thing I had learned from my training, it was that you should never make the first strike. All it does is gives the other person the advantage because they just block your strike and then they strike you back, and only a very experienced fighter would be able to block that.

When the bear's sword touched mine, I sent a small electric shock to the bear, just enough to stun it. In the split second that it was stunned, I sliced it across the stomach, but that was all I had time to do. If I had tried to slice its leg, like I usually would have done, it would have had enough time to recover, and it would have struck me on the head or back.

Nobody can beat me in a duel. I was trained by the best, and I am the most powerful fighter in the world. Why would I let an insignificant bear end my life?

The bear had a line of blood across its stomach, and no longer had the ability to fight.

What a weak animal! Just one cut and it can't fight anymore! Do these animals even get trained for battle?

The bear fell to its knees and pleaded me not to kill it. I gave in to its plea, and decided not to kill it. It's not like it could do anything to anyone anyways. I walked away from it and closer to the front of the castle. While I was walking closer, I saw that the battle was over. Not one fox lay dead or wounded, and more than half of the other side's army was wounded or dead.

I took my army inside the castle, to claim victory. I also told the survivors to come with me, because they would be held as prisoners. I walked to the king's chamber in the castle, and went and sat on the chair. It was a very nice castle and it now it belonged to me. I had been waiting for that moment of victory for so long, you would not believe it.

"Warriors, you have done our nation a great favor today. We have finally defeated the wolves! All of you who fought today will become great heroes, and you can never be thanked enough for what you have done. And those of you who survived from the wolves' side of the army, I will give you one chance. If you join us in our quest, you will not be harmed, but if you do not, you will become our prisoners. Those of you who wish to join, please come to the front," I said.

Only about ten survivors came up front, half were monkeys; the others were deer, and wolves. "Those of you who do not wish to join me, follow me to the dungeon."

The Conquering

I walked out of the king's room and over to the hidden door in the ground. The rest of the survivors followed me to the dungeon, and I locked them all in their own cells.

I looked around the entire castle, and there seemed to be all of one thing missing. *Where in the world was Kevdak?*

WE FIGURE OUT THE RIDDLE

Rick

I walked over to the castle with Aric's backpack on my back and my sword on my side. I saw everyone waiting for me. Xavier, Alex and Roy were all standing in front of the castle talking about something. There was nobody else outside the castle, well nobody living anyway. There were a bunch of animals' bodies lying dead in front of the castle. There was nothing but grass in all directions of the castle for about half a mile. I wondered what had happened there.

We Figure Out the Riddle

I bet they all found their orbs. I guess I'll have to face them and see what they say. If they did find their orbs, they would be able to help me get to mine.

"Hey," I said.

"Did you find your orb?" asked Alex.

"No," I replied with my head drooping down, feeling ashamed.

"Come on! Am I seriously the only one that found my orb?" asked Xavier.

Huh? "What do you mean? Did Roy and Alex not find their orbs either?"

"No. I found out that my map wasn't exactly a map. It was a sheet of paper with a stupid riddle on it that I couldn't figure out," said Alex.

"And when I went to the place my map was pointing to, there was a cave that had really unstable ground. If I had stepped inside, I probably would have died," said Roy.

"Wow. I was about to climb up the mountain that my orb was on, but there was a huge blizzard that I couldn't have survived in," I said, "Oh, and I have another question, what happened here?"

Chapter Fourteen

"Well, after we left, it seems like Bailey and his stupid army of foxes went up against the wolves' army, and they won," said Xavier.

"If we all had our orbs right now, we could all go in there and beat him up, but Aric hid the orbs so that we might die while trying to get them," complained Roy.

"I got my orb, Aric didn't make it that hard for me."

"Well you're just...you."

"I wish Aric was still alive so we could ask him how to get our orbs."

After Alex said that, I realized that I had found something out that probably nobody else knew about, and I completely forgot about it: Aric Johnson was still alive. *Why didn't I ask him that?* I wondered, *I guess it just didn't cross my mind.*

"I forgot to tell you something really important that I found out. Aric actually *is* alive," I said.

"Yeah, like we're going to believe that," said Xavier.

"You should!"

"Where's your proof? How do we know that you're not just trying to trick us?" asked Alex.

We Figure Out the Riddle

"Um…" I then remembered that I still had Aric's backpack on, "Oh! Was I wearing this backpack when I left?"

"Not that I recall," said Roy, "I bet it magically appeared on your back yesterday," then they all started laughing.

"No it didn't! I met Aric and he gave me his backpack to borrow!"

"Fine, that's enough proof, I'll believe you, but how's that going to help us?" asked Xavier.

"It's not, but now that we're together, we have to find the orbs so that we can defeat Bailey," I said.

"Nice idea, but who's orb do we find first?" asked Alex.

It was a great question, and we discussed it for a while, and we finally came to a conclusion. It was Xavier's idea, like it would usually be; Lauren and he are the ideas people.

"So it's settled," said Xavier, "we have to figure out Alex's stupid riddle, and then find the orb."

"Wait, shouldn't we go someplace safer to do all this?" asked Roy, "Because Bailey could step out any second and blow us all up with his awesome lightning powers."

"He has a point you know," said Alex.

"Where do we go?" I asked.

"We should go near the portal, or even to Wolf Mountain, just to be safe," said Xavier while pointing in the direction of the portal.

We walked to the portal and decided that the best option would be to go to Wolf Mountain. The forest around the portal had been completely burned down. It was horrible, but like I had learned in science, a forest fire would make the forest soil more fertile, and it would grow back better than ever, so I still had hope for that place.

When we got to Wolf Mountain, I looked around and saw the beautiful pond was still shinning because the sunlight was bouncing off of it so that it sparkled. The place was still as great as I had remembered it, and after looking closely, I saw that our stuff was still there from when we had came right before Kevdak pulled us into Neosolgis. Our tent was standing up and our sleeping bags were probably still sitting inside.

We Figure Out the Riddle

I walked over to the tent and everyone else followed me. I went inside and sat down on my sleeping bag. The tent barely had enough room to fit five sleeping bags, so it was perfect for us. Roy, Alex, and Xavier all sat down on their sleeping bags too.

"So Alex," said Roy, "what's this riddle you were telling us about?"

"Well, I read it so many times trying to figure it out, so I have it memorized. The riddle on the map is; hot or cold when nations unite, those five circles are their might, yet without this flame there shall be no game."

"Hmm…" I said, thinking of what the riddle could possibly be referring to.

"I have no idea," said Xavier, "anyone else have any ideas?"

"Nope," I said.

"Not a clue," said Roy.

"Maybe we could find Lauren and ask her, she's always been good at solving puzzles and riddles," said Alex.

"That's a great idea," said Xavier.

"To Eve's house!" announced Roy.

Chapter Fourteen

"Wait, why Eve's house?" I asked.

"That's where you told Lauren to go, right?" asked Xavier.

"Oh, right," I had forgotten that I told her to go there.

We walked down the mountain and went straight to Eve's house. It took about half an hour to get there, and the whole time, I was thinking about the riddles. I couldn't seem to figure out what it was saying. *Since Aric had been in Neosolgis when Corvyre told him to hide the orbs, it probably has something to do with the animals, but why would the foxes and wolves ever unite for something? Oh well, Lauren will be able to figure it out.*

When we got there, it was about three in the afternoon, so we were all tired and sweaty. I went up to Eve's house and rang the doorbell. Eve opened the door with her long hair running over her shoulders and the sunlight made it look almost brown. She was wearing jeans, like she usually does, and she wasn't looking as stressed out as she had looked the last time we saw her.

"I was wondering when you guys would get here," she said, "Lauren told me what happened. Did you all get your orbs yet? Because if you did, I can give Lauren her map, and you guys can go find her orb."

"No, only Xavier found his orb, and the reason we came here is because we need Lauren to help us figure something out," I said.

"Oh, then come in," said Eve while moving out of the doorway so we could enter.

When I walked inside, I looked around at her house. I noticed things I had never paid attention to. The walls were a medium shade of brown, and they looked really bumpy. There were paintings hung on the walls, they were mostly of nature and such. When you first step into the house, you enter the living room, which was where Lauren was. On all sides of the living room, there were brown leather couches that could fit three people each.

Lauren was sitting on the couch on the left side and she got up as soon as she saw us walk inside the room. "What's wrong?" she asked. Once again, with that weird ability of hers, she could immediately tell something was wrong.

"We need your help," said Alex as we all went to sit down. Eve sat down too, and she was right next to me.

Chapter Fourteen

"What do you need my help with?" asked Lauren while sitting back down.

"Well there's something I never noticed about my map," said Alex looking ashamed, "it's not exactly a map."

"Then what is it?" asked Lauren.

"All it has on it a riddle that, sadly, none of us can figure out" said Xavier, "So we came here because we know you're great at solving things like this."

"What's the riddle exactly?" asked Eve.

"Hot or cold when nations unite, those five circles are their might, yet without this flame there shall be no game."

"What does that mean?" asked Eve; she seemed really anxious to figure it out.

"Hmm," Lauren sat there for a while, looking into space muttering things to herself, like she always does when she's in deep thought.

"Seriously?" she asked, "This is pretty simple, once you think about it."

We Figure Out the Riddle

"We did, but we don't know anything about nations uniting, or about what games animals would play!" said Alex.

"You really need to start learning how to think outside the box," said Lauren, like the answer was the most obvious thing in the world.

"Are you going to tell us the answer or not?" asked Eve impatiently.

"I will, but first, I'll let you get to the answer by yourselves," said Lauren.

"Do we have to?" complained Roy.

"Yes," answered Lauren, "Let me tell you why it's so obvious. OK, what's the first thing that comes to your mind when you think of a flame, five circles, games, and nations uniting in the hot or cold?"

"The Olympics!" shouted Eve.

"Exactly, all you guys were doing wrong was that you were thinking of the wrong world," said Lauren.

"Oh," I said, feeling stupid. *Why is it that Eve and Lauren could easily figure it out, but I couldn't? I need to start thinking harder.*

Chapter Fourteen

"So what does it have to do with the Olympics?" asked Xavier.

"I believe it's talking about the Olympic torch," said Lauren.

"Wait, are you telling me that you think the orb is inside the Olympic torch?" asked Alex.

"Yup, I think that's pretty much what she's saying," said Eve.

"Why do you think it's inside the Olympic torch?" I asked.

"Well, think about it, what else that has to do with the Olympics has to do with fire? And it makes sense, the fire orb has probably been the reason the fire in the torch has been going on for years without stopping," said Lauren.

"So are you saying that we're going to have to steal the Olympic torch?" I asked.

"Yeah, I think that's the only thing we can do," responded Lauren.

"That's crazy!" exclaimed Roy, "How on earth are we supposed to get the Olympic torch?!"

We Figure Out the Riddle

"Wait, but, isn't it the flame that's passed from runner to runner?" asked Xavier, "I thought that every torchbearer has a torch or their own."

"Well if that's true, then where's the orb?" I asked.

"Well, I remember reading somewhere that there's an eternal flame that's used for the Olympic flame in the temple of Hestia," said Xavier.

"That's just an urban legend," said Lauren, "they just light the first torch in the temple of Hestia in honor of the original Olympic Games."

"Well, there's no harm in trying," said Alex.

"Great, where is it?" asked Roy.

"In Olympia," responded Xavier.

"You mean the city in Washington?" asked Alex.

"No, I mean in Greece."

"How are we supposed to get to Greece?!" I exclaimed.

"Maybe we could go ask Eve's dad, he was the one who hid the orbs in the first place," said Roy.

"How would you ask my dad? He's probably dead," said Eve.

Chapter Fourteen

"Yeah," said Lauren, "there's no way out of this, we have to go to Greece."

"Not entirely," said Xavier, "Rick said that he met Eve's dad while he was trying to find his orb."

"You shouldn't have said that," I mumbled, but no one heard me.

"What?!" screamed Eve, "My dad's been alive this *whole* time and he never came back to see me or my mom?! When I see him, I'll-"

"Eve," I cut her off, "I don't think it's the best idea for you to go to Neosolgis, especially at this dangerous of a time."

"What's so dangerous that's going on there that I can't handle, huh?"

"Well, there's this guy that can control lightning and he and his army of foxes just took over the wolves' kingdom, so it's dangerous for anyone to be there, plus, he wants to kill us so we would be taking a risk just going there. And if you come along, there's more of a chance that someone will get hurt," I said.

"So what? I haven't seen my dad in seven years! If your dad had been gone for seven years, then you suddenly find out he's alive, wouldn't you want to see him?" asked Eve.

"I guess so," I admitted.

"So, will you let me go with you?"

"Fine, you can come."

"So, where are we going?" asked Lauren.

"We have to go back to the other world," I said while getting up.

"Lead the way, Rick," said Xavier, "it's time to see if Eve's dad really is still alive."

I walked out of Eve's house, and everyone followed me. It was the first time in a while that all six of us were together. Eve walked up next to me and whispered, "Thanks for letting me come."

"No problem," I whispered back.

Everyone was talking to someone else the whole way there, and we weren't paying attention to anything. Lauren was talking to Alex, Xavier was talking to Roy, and I was talking to Eve. Finally, when we were all about to go through the portal, we all quieted down. We walked through the bush one by one, and I was the first one to go.

Chapter Fourteen

"What happened here?" asked Eve as soon as we got to the other side of the bush, "This is nothing like the last time I was here."

"It's a long story, but basically, the guy who could control lightning came here with his army of foxes and destroyed the whole place, then he took over the castle from the inside," I paused for a second, "Wow, that sentence wouldn't have made any sense a month ago."

"OK then," she said, probably really confused.

"Where do we go now, mister guide person?" asked Roy.

"Well, it'll be pretty obvious once we're going in the right direction," I said.

"And what direction would that be?" asked Xavier.

"That way," I said while pointing in the direction my orb was in. I started walking that way, and we all started talking again. We talked for so long, and about so many different things, I don't even remember what Eve and I were talking about.

It took about an hour or two before we could see the outline of the giant tree. Once I could see it, the sun was starting to go down. I started speed walking so we would get there faster. It took a lot less time to get there than it had the last time.

The wooden cabin was still there, and the tree was too. I knocked on the door and I heard a voice from inside muttering something. I looked at Eve's face, and it was filled with excitement. As Aric opened the door, I heard everyone whisper to each other, and Eve was staring at her dad in awe, and it seemed like she was starting to cry.

"What's this?" he said, "You brought your friends along for a friendly visit?"

"Actually, there's something we need to ask you, and someone we need to show you," I said.

"Who is it that you want to show me?"

"Someone you'll definitely recognize," I said while looking at Eve. Aric also looked at Eve, and he looked shocked.

"Eve?" he whispered.

"It's me," she replied. Eve ran up to her dad and gave him a hug, and he hugged her back.

"You don't know how much I've missed you," she said while crying and looking up to her dad's face.

Chapter Fourteen

"I missed you too," said Aric. After about a minute, he let go of Eve, looked at her, and said, "You were so small last time I saw you, look at you now. Why don't you all come in, and we can talk."

Aric turned around and walked inside. We all followed him to the room that I had been talking to him on my last visit. We all sat down on the couches; Eve sat next to her dad, and everyone else got a couch to themselves.

"So, what is it you want to ask me?"

"Well, it's about the fire orb," I said, "we think that it's in the temple of Hestia in Olympia, Greece, and we want to know if we're right."

"It is. I see you solved the riddle, but you came all this way just to see if you were right?"

"Yeah, but there's something else too," said Lauren.

"And what's that?" asked Aric.

"How in the world do we get to Greece without getting on a plane?" asked Roy.

"Think about it," said Aric, "how did you get here?"

"By walking here," said Xavier.

"I meant how you got to Neosolgis."

We Figure Out the Riddle

"Through the portal," said Eve.

"Exactly, so think of how big both of the worlds are, and do you think that the only portal between both the worlds is atop Wolf Mountain?"

"So you're saying that there's another portal that leads to Greece?" asked Lauren.

"Exactly," said Aric.

"So where's this other portal?" I asked.

"It is nowhere you haven't been," said Aric, "it's around the mountain where the air orb is. I found it when I was hiding the orb."

"OK thanks," said Roy, "I guess we'll be leaving now."

"Oh, wait," I said, "I have one last thing to do." I got up, walked towards Aric, and gave him his backpack back.

"I hope it served you well," said Aric.

"It did."

We started walking out, and I noticed that Eve stayed sitting. "Aren't you coming?" I asked her.

"No, I'll stay here with my dad," she responded.

Chapter Fourteen

"Well, see you later then," I said, while waving goodbye to both of them.

We all walked outside and I started walking in the direction that the mountains were in. After walking for a few hours, it got dark enough to the point that we could barely see anymore, so we all went to sleep. Lauren and Xavier were the lucky ones, they could use their quivers as pillows, but Roy, Alex and I were stuck sleeping on the grass.

Once we were all awake, we started walking again, because we needed to get to Greece as fast as possible. When we got there, I looked around for another portal. The sad thing was that it would take forever to look around an entire mountain in one group.

"We should split up," I said.

"Split up? Why?" asked Lauren.

"So that we'll be able to find the other portal faster, obviously," said Xavier.

"Exactly," I said.

"So which way do we go?" asked Roy.

"Two of us go one way; the other three go the other way."

We Figure Out the Riddle

I walked around the left side of the mountain, and Lauren and Alex followed me. They were a few feet behind me, and they were having their own little conversation. Without Eve with me, there was nobody to talk to because Lauren and Alex would always be in a conversation, and so would Xavier and Roy.

We walked around the mountain for quite some time, seeing as it was a pretty big mountain. When we finally got to the other side, Roy and Xavier were coming around the other side. On the exact other side of where we had started from, was another giant bush.

"I guess when Aric said around the mountain, he literally meant *around* the mountain," said Roy.

"So do we just step through the bush?" asked Alex.

"I guess so," I replied. I walked up to the bush, parted the branches, and stepped through it.

Chapter Fifteen

RANDOMLY STEPPING INTO GREECE

Rick

When I stepped out, I was in an entirely different place. The portals were amazing; they could take you from one world to another without any difficulty. I started to wonder how they worked, but it just boggled my mind.

It was nice to be back in the world I came from, yet I still had no idea where I was. In front of me, there were the ruins of what probably used to be a Greek temple of some sort. There was a pure white rectangular floor that took up about 2,500 square feet. There were only a few pillars left standing, and a few of them were only half the height of a regular pillar. The temple had probably been eroded away through the centuries because it was at a high elevation.

"I thought you said there would be an eternal flame here," Roy said.

"That's what I've heard," said Xavier.

"I told you that it's just an urban legend," said Lauren.

"So which one is true?" asked Alex.

"I'm going to go with Lauren because there's no evidence of an eternal flame here," I said.

"That's true, but how do we know we're in the right place?" asked Xavier. I guess we were all arguing because we all hate to be wrong about anything.

"How do we find out if this *is* the right place?" I asked.

"Let's go ask one of the locals," Lauren said while motioning to the large city below us. I looked down and all I could see were houses. There were roads going through the neighborhoods, and the streets were in a very organized fashion. It reminded me of America, but there was something distinctly different about Greece. I couldn't tell what it was, but it was definitely there.

Chapter Fifteen

There were a lot less cars on the road than there would be in America, and there were a lot more people walking to places. It was a bright and peaceful day outside; a perfect day to hang out outside.

We walked down the small hill and entered the neighborhood. I looked around for someone that looked friendly that we could talk to. There was a man walking on the sidewalk who looked like he would be a nice guy. He was wearing blue jeans and a white t-shirt. He had very short, dark brown hair; almost the exact color of mine. The guy looked like he was just enjoying the nice day and taking a walk.

"Excuse me," I said to him, "can you help us?"

"If I am guessing correctly you must be visiting from America, I say that because of your USA t-shirt and your accent, how can I help you?" he said with a Greek accent.

"We were just wondering where the Temple of Hestia is," I said.

"Ah, you see that hill up there?" he asked while pointing to the hill we had just come down from.

"Yeah," I said.

"Just at the top are the ruins of the Temple of Hestia. I hope I have been of assistance," he said.

"You have, thank you," I replied

"Good day," he said, and then walked away.

"OK, so if that's the temple of Hestia, and there's no eternal flame, then where's the orb?" asked Xavier.

"Let's go back up there and see if we can find something helpful," said Lauren. With that, we headed back up to the Temple of Hestia, and walked around, looking for anything that could help us in any way, shape, or form.

I was walking around, and in the center, I saw some stones that were slightly raised from the ground. I bent down so I could look at them more closely. There were four of them, they were all squares and in the shape of a plus sign, but there wasn't a stone in the center.

"You might want to see this," I said.

"What is it?" asked Roy.

"Come over here and you'll find out," I said while standing back up.

"I don't see anything," said Roy, looking confused.

Chapter Fifteen

"Look closely," I said, "there's four stones that are raised from the ground, maybe we have to press them in a pattern."

"Maybe, but how would we know the pattern?" asked Lauren.

"Wait Alex, can I see your paper with the riddle on it for a second?" I asked.

"Sure," he said. Alex handed me the folded paper out of her pocket, and I unfolded it. I looked at both sides of the wrinkled, brown piece of paper over and over, looking for something that would indicate the pattern. I couldn't seem to find anything, but then I remembered something. Maybe Aric had put a watermark on it. I held it up to the sun, and there it was, at the bottom right corner of the paper. It said *left, left, right, up, down, right, right, up, up, down, left.*

"There!" I exclaimed, while pointing to the faint watermark I had found.

"Someone press them in that combination!" said Xavier.

"I'll do it," said Alex. We all moved away from the spot where the stones were, and Alex stayed there and pushed them in the combination it said. Once she was done, there was a loud sound that sounded like large rocks moving and scraping against each other. Alex moved back to where we were as the ground around the spot where the stones were was being pushed back. The slab of rock that moved was about ten feet wide, ten feet long, and one foot thick. When it moved aside, there was a small stairway leading to a cave directly under the temple. *I wonder if anyone else besides Aric has ever found this place.*

"Whoa," I said in wonder. *I guess it's still possible that there's an eternal flame somewhere down there.*

"So do we go down there, or what?" asked Roy.

"What else do we have to do?" I asked.

"Let's go," said Lauren.

"Hey Alex," I started, "can you make a small flame so we can see down there?"

"No problem," she replied calmly. She opened the palm of her right hand upwards and a small flame started floating about a centimeter above her hand. With Alex leading the way, we walked down the steps, and into the creepy cave that came out of nowhere.

Chapter Fifteen

When we were all in the cave, I could see only a few feet in front of me because Alex's flame was so small. From what I could see, there were spider webs on the walls, and the place looked ancient. The walls were brown; the shade of dirt, and were cracked in a few places. The tunnel went on forever, taking random turns and it didn't seem like we were getting anywhere.

"Isn't this where we started?" asked Roy.

"I think so," I said while looking around, because it looked like the same place.

"Wait," said Lauren, "I think this is some kind labyrinth."

"And what makes you say that?" asked Xavier.

"Well just think about it, this place is under a Greek temple, and it was probably made in the times of ancient Greece. The Greek had myths and legends about a guy named Daedalus, who built the Labyrinth, which was an endless maze that only he knew how to navigate. So maybe to protect the Olympic flame, which was in honor of the god Zeus, they built a fake labyrinth to protect it," reasoned Lauren.

"Or maybe Aric built it to make people get lost down here," said Roy.

"It makes a lot of sense, but that just puts us in a worse situation than we're already in," I said.

"So what do we do?" asked Alex.

"The only thing we can do, we find the orb," said Lauren.

"And how do we do that?" asked Xavier.

"I remember that in one myth about the Labyrinth, someone got to the center by always turning right," Lauren said, trying to be helpful.

"You really think that'll work?" I asked doubtfully.

"What other option do we have?" asked Lauren.

"So, are we going to go now?" asked Xavier impatiently.

"I guess so," I said.

With my last comment, Alex turned right at the first hallway, rather than going straight, like we had done before. The next turn came not too long after, and so did the next one. I was keeping a mental map of where we had been, so that we would be able to get out if we ever needed to. We went from turn after turn after turn, and after a while, I could see a faint light coming from around the corner.

"There it is!" I shouted. We started running to the light, and we took a right turn. When we came around the corner, we finally came to a room. It was as small as the average bedroom, and in the middle, was a stone fireplace. It was as tall as the ceiling, which I could see for the first time, and there was a whole through the middle in where there was a giant flame. We walked up to the flame, and I could feel the heat coming from it.

Alex walked around it, and she told us to come to the other side. "What is it?" I asked, but right then, I saw it, her orb. It was sitting in a small hole that was a little bit bigger than itself. It was crystal clear, except that on the inside there was a small flame, it looked like it was actually burning inside of it. Alex looked at it for a second, and then she picked it up with her left hand while still staring at it in awe. We were all awe-struck by it, except Xavier. He already had his orb, so it wasn't a big deal to him. The moment Alex took the orb out of its place, the fire shrunk a little bit. We all stepped back as soon as it happened, but we were fine.

"Put it in your sword, see what happens," said Roy excitedly.

"Sure," she responded. Alex took out her sword, and it shinned in the light from the fire. She held it up in front of her face, and put the orb in from the bottom. Slowly, starting from the bottom of the blade, the sword caught on fire, strike that, it turned *into* fire. We all backed away from Alex with our hands up, it was our natural reaction from fire. There was no metal left on the blade anymore, but when Alex moved the sword around, the fire didn't get blown by the wind, it stayed in place, but it still looked like it was burning. The fire was almost like a solid object.

"Cool," said Alex and Roy at the same time, amazed.

"No fair!" shouted Xavier, "Nothing happened to my bow when I put my orb in!"

"Too bad," said Alex.

"So how do you feel, now that you have your orb?" I asked.

"Powerful," she said, "I feel like I can do anything, like I'm unstoppable."

Chapter Fifteen

"That's great, but we should really get going now," said Xavier.

"Sure, but what do I do with my sword now?" asked Alex.

"Try sheathing it," I suggested as I shrugged my shoulders. She touched the tip of the blade to the inside of the sheath, and it immediately turned back into a regular steel sword. Alex's eyes widened as she saw that happen.

"Let's go," said Xavier impatiently.

"All right, Alex you lead the way, all we have to do is turn left now," I said, "and hopefully you can give us a bigger flame this time."

"No problem," she said. Then, she made a huge flame erupt out of her hand, and she almost burnt herself.

"Sorry, I guess I don't know my own strength yet," she immediately shrunk the flame to a reasonable size; so that she wouldn't burn herself, but we could still see clearly.

It took us a while to get out of the labyrinth, but at least we could see a lot better that time. Once we got out, my eyes started burning because it was so bright out and I had been so used to being in a dark, underground cave.

"Well, one orb down, three to go," I said, really not wanting to have to go through that, or something worse, three more times.

We walked around the place where the ground had moved, and we decided to push it back to its original state. It took all five of us pushing as hard as we could to move it. Once we pushed it, the slab of stone clicked into place.

"That took a lot longer than I thought it would," said Alex.

We walked over to the portal, and walked through. Right before I went back, I turned around and took one last look at Greece.

WE GET INTO A BLIZZARD

Rick

When I stepped out of the portal, we were next to the mountain, the exact same place we needed to be. "Well this makes things a lot easier," I said, happy that we didn't need go anywhere else to get my orb.

"So what now, do we all just climb up the mountain?" asked Roy.

"I think that the only people that should go up there are the people who have to," said Xavier, "from here, it looks really dangerous, and we shouldn't risk us all going up there."

"So who's going?" asked Alex.

We Get Into a Blizzard

"Well, when I was here before, I realized that three people need to go up there; me, Alex and Xavier."

"When do we leave?" asked Xavier.

"Now's a better time than any, we've not a moment to lose," I said.

"What do Lauren and I do while you're gone?" asked Roy. He sounded disappointed about something; it was either that he wouldn't have Xavier to talk to or that he couldn't go with us.

"Just stay here and wait for us to come back," I said.

"But can't it be dangerous if we stay here?" asked Roy, "Because if the foxes come and attack us, we're almost defenseless because Lauren and I haven't found our orbs yet."

"He's got a point," said Alex.

"Fine," I said, "you can come."

"Yes!" shouted Roy.

We all walked around to the other side of the mountain so we could climb up. The mountain was definitely a lot taller than Wolf Mountain; I could tell for two reasons, there was snow at the top and it just looked a lot bigger. I looked up, wondering how long it might take us to get to the very top.

"How long do you think it'll take to get to the top?" I asked.

"Definitely more than twenty-four hours," replied Lauren.

"Well, there's no time to lose, let's get going," I said while starting to walk closer to the mountain. We started up the large, barren mountain and I braced myself for what was coming up. Luckily for us, there was a trail that leads straight to the top. The only bad part was that it swirled up the mountain like a slithering snake.

I was in the front, and Xavier and Alex were directly behind me. Usually, we would travel as a group, but the trail was only wide enough for one person to be on at a time, otherwise you would fall off the side of the mountain to your doom. We obviously didn't want that happening, so we stayed in a single file line, like your first grade teacher would tell you to do after recess.

The higher we went up, the colder it got; it felt good for the first hour or two because it was a really warm day outside, but soon I had started to wish I had been smart enough to bring a jacket or sweatshirt.

"How long is this going to take?" asked Roy. He would always find something to complain about.

"However long it takes for us to get there," I said, trying to get him to stop complaining.

"How long will that be?" he asked.

Just to get him to quiet down, I said, "About fifteen hours."

"Dang it!"

Another hour passed, and I was starting to get really cold, but it wasn't snowing or raining. "Hey Alex, is there any way you can warm us up?"

"Sure, but I'm not sure I can keep a fire moving while we walk, but if we stop for a little bit, I can make a fire easily," she said. I looked around for a place where we could all sit around a campfire, and I saw a ledge not too far from where we were. I kept walking, and I soon saw that it crossed the trail we were following.

"Right here!" I shouted excitedly. We all sat down in a circle and Alex made a big fire in the middle. I put my hands up so they would get warm faster, and everyone else did the same thing. "So when do we start going again?" asked Ray anxiously.

"Whenever everyone's warm enough," I said.

A few minutes passed and Roy asked, "Is everyone warm now?"

"I'm good," I said.

"Same," said Xavier. Everyone else agreed, and we got back to going up the mountain. An hour passed, and it started snowing; the bad thing was that we were all wearing shorts and t-shirts.

"Hey Alex, now might be the time to learn how to make a fire move while we walk," I said while my teeth chattered and I shivered.

"I'll try my best," she said. She made a wall of fire around all of us, and it felt great to be warm again. Alex also made it smaller in the front so we could still see where we were going; one reason I didn't like being in the front. We had all stopped for a few seconds, waiting for Alex to make the fire, and once she did, I took a small step forward. When everyone else had moved, the fire moved too. She *did it!* I thought, *now we don't have to worry about freezing to death!* The only problem was that snow could still fall on us from above, but it would melt after a few seconds. Seeing Alex's powers made me anxious to get my orb.

Not very long after, there started to be a lot of snow on the ground, and Alex's wall of fire was melting it as we passed over it. It was all fine until the water started to put out the fire.

"Xavier!" I shouted over the howling winds.

"What?" he shouted.

"Can you move the water so it doesn't put out the fire?!"

"I'll try, but I need to be in the front so I can see the water!"

"Okay!" apparently Alex had heard our conversation because she immediately made the fire on both sides of Xavier and I disappear so we could switch places. We both turned sideways and moved past each other and then faced forward again. Xavier made the water into a ball, made it float in the air and then threw it off the side of the mountain. He had to keep on doing this over and over because we had to keep moving, and the snow kept getting melted.

Chapter Sixteen

The weather just kept getting worse, and that just made it harder to make it to the top. Luckily, we all made it there alive. The top of the mountain was flat, small and snowy. We still needed the fire to keep us warm, so Alex kept it going. I soon realized that it got a lot harder to breathe because we were at such a high elevation, and it wasn't helping that we had a huge fire burning up a lot of our precious oxygen.

I could barely see, but from what I could tell from the light of the fire, there was something round and shiny sitting in the middle of the peak. Since we were on flat ground, our single file line turned into a group again. I walked forward, and I told Alex to let me out of the ring of fire for a few seconds so I could grab my orb.

I ran out, grabbed the orb and ran back in. The moment I touched the orb, I was filled with energy. I didn't feel tired at all anymore; it was the most amazing things that ever happened to me. I would have stood there forever, but I remembered that we would probably die from lack of oxygen if we stood there any longer.

We turned around and headed back down the trail. After a few minutes, I could breathe normally again.

We Get Into a Blizzard

Xavier was still in the front because he needed to move all of the melted snow out of our way so we would stay warm and we wouldn't slip and fall.

It took a few hours, but we were finally out of the snow. It was still cold, but we could see a lot better and we didn't have to rely on Alex's fire as much.

"I can't believe we already have three orbs!" I said.

"Yeah, but none of them are mine," muttered Roy. I'm not sure if anyone else heard him, because nobody said anything after that. We finally got to the point that we didn't need the fire anymore and somehow it was still sunny outside. I was trying to figure it out, and I finally did when I remembered what Lauren had said just before we started going up the mountain. *Definitely more than twenty-four hours.*

Has it really been a whole day since we left? I wondered, *it's definitely possible, I just didn't think that it would actually take that long.*

By the time I was done thinking, we were at the bottom of the mountain, at last.

Chapter Seventeen

ROY IS FINALLY SATISFIED

Alex

"Do we get to go find my orb now?" asked Roy after we all woke up from a few hours of sleep in the middle of the day and had eaten some food.

"Yes, we get to go find yours next," said Lauren.

"Finally!" he exclaimed, "do you know how long I've been waiting for us to be able to go find my orb?"

"It's been a while," I agreed.

"Can we leave now so we can get there faster?" he pleaded.

"Sure, let's go," I said. I think I was speaking for everyone seeing as we had all had some sleep and food;

so we were all energized and ready to go. I then remembered that I forgot to do something that Alex had done in the labyrinth under the Temple of Hestia.

Remembering that, I took my sword out of its sheath from where it was placed on grass next to where I had been sleeping. Next, I picked up the orb from where I had placed it the previous night, and put it in the bottom of the hilt of my sword. As soon as it clicked in position, the hilt of my sword slowly started to turn into a small tornado. The weird thing was that it still felt completely solid in my hand.

"Awesome," I said to myself. Personally, I thought that Alex's sword turning into fire was cooler than what my sword did until a saw a small tornado at the tip of my sword too. It was less than half the size of the hilt. When I put my sword back in its sheath, the hilt turned back to normal again.

"So are we going or what?" asked Roy very impatiently.

"Yeah, let's go," I replied, "wait, where are we going anyways?"

"It's a mountain not far from here," said Roy.

Chapter Seventeen

"We have to climb up another mountain?" asked Alex.

"Actually, it's in a cave under the mountain," said Roy.

It's a good thing too; I'd never want to climb a mountain that big again.

"Lead the way, Roy," said Xavier.

"This way," said Roy. He led us down the mountain range and it took forever. The scenery wasn't changing, and it only got hotter during the day. Nothing particularly exciting happened on the way there, so I won't bore you to death with the details.

When we got there, I couldn't tell if we were even at the correct mountain or not, but apparently Roy could. "This is the place!" shouted Roy.

"And where are we exactly?" asked Xavier.

"This is the mountain, and there should be a cave somewhere and in there is the orb," he responded. He took us around the mountain, and there was a cave. From the inside, there was a deep rumbling.

"What's that sound?" I asked.

Roy is Finally Satisfied

"That's the only reason that I couldn't get the orb by myself," said Roy, "the cave is filled with shaky ground; I would have died if I had stepped in there."

"So how are we supposed to help?" asked Xavier.

"I don't know, I was just saying that I can't do this by myself."

"Maybe since it's too dark to see much in there, Alex can make a fire," I suggested.

"That would help," said Lauren.

"Should we all go inside?" asked Alex. It was a great question, but one of the few I didn't have an answer for.

"It's not a bad idea, for the same reason we all went to find Rick's orb," said Lauren.

"I guess we're all going then?" asked Alex.

"Yup, seems like it," I said.

"Cool, so are we going now?" asked Roy.

"Okay," I said, "if anyone has any objections, speak now or forever hold your peace," nobody said anything, so I assumed we were all going at that moment. Alex led us into the cave holding a fire in her hand like she had done in the labyrinth.

Chapter Seventeen

We walked forward very carefully, looking at the ground every step of the way. We would step over cracks like little kids that still believed the superstition *step on a crack and you break your mom's back*. It was pretty hard, because there were cracks everywhere. In some places, the ground was actually shaking, making it a lot harder to avoid all of the cracks. At one point, I almost fell because of the shaky ground, but Xavier saved me. "Thanks," I said softly.

"Anytime," was his reply.

We got really far into the cave, and the farther we went, the shakier the ground got. Once, the ground suddenly got really shaky so we all fell down. The ground then started to break apart, creating large abysses everywhere. There was an abyss all around us, and we were all sitting on the same island. Apparently our fall had been enough to trigger the small amount of force that was needed to break the ground apart. The noise got so loud that I could barely hear anything other than the ground shaking and I had to scream at the top of my lung so the others could hear me.

"What do we do now?!" I screamed.

Roy is Finally Satisfied

"We keep going!" Roy shouted back at me.

"How?!" asked Xavier.

"We jump!" shouted Roy.

"That's crazy!" shouted Lauren.

"What else can we do?!" asked Roy.

Since we were stuck on an island of ground, we had nowhere else to go, unless we went back, which would have been just as dangerous and would have defeated the purpose of us going in the cave in the first place. We all took turns jumping across the three foot wide abyss and to the next island; it was scarier than you would think. Luckily, we all made it across the first few, but there were always more, no matter how far we went. At one point, I was the last one to jump, and when my foot was on the next island, I slipped. Xavier was right in front of me, and he had cat-like reflexes so he grabbed onto my arms and pulled me up. The next island was farther away from the one we were on than any of the other islands of stone.

"So, who wants to go first?" asked Alex. I know what you're thinking; I went first because I'm the brave one, the leader, but if there's one thing I'm afraid of, it's plummeting to my certain death in a rumbling cave.

Chapter Seventeen

"I'll go first," said Roy. I guess he was being brave because…well I don't really know. He took a small running start, and jumped across the abyss with his left foot forward. He barely landed on the ledge with his left foot, and I let out a breath I didn't know I was holding. Just when he was about to step on with both feet, the island shook a little bit and Roy lost his balance and fell over.

"Roy!" I shouted. I almost started crying, and I understood how Aric must have felt when he found out that his friends had died. We all started yelling his name in hopes that he would still be alive. *This is all my fault,* I thought, *I shouldn't have let him jump, it's too dangerous.*

I had just run out of hope when I heard a voice come from below, "guys! I'm still alive!" the bottom's only about ten feet from where you're standing!" *He's not dead?!* I thought to myself.

"Is there anything down there?" asked Xavier.

"I'll just come up and show you!" said Roy.

"How are are you going to get back up here?" asked Alex.

Roy is Finally Satisfied

"You'll see!" Roy suddenly appeared from the ground, and he was standing on rock that wasn't there before. I was suddenly confused, and I was guessing everyone else was too. Roy looked ecstatic; a bit too happy for someone who had just fallen down a ten-foot deep hole.

"Did you hit your head down there?" asked Xavier, "because..."

Roy cut him off, "I found my orb down there!"

"Down there, how?" asked Lauren.

"Well, when I fell down there, I noticed a little shiny thing in the corner. I got up, and grabbed it. It was round, and I realized that it was what I had been looking for," said Roy.

"So you found the orb?" asked Alex.

"Yeah, and I also realized that when I picked it up, the earthquakes stopped."

I hadn't noticed that. I had been too busy thinking of what happened to Roy, "Well that makes it a whole lot easier to get out," I said.

"Yup," said Roy.

"What are we waiting for exactly?" asked Xavier.

Chapter Seventeen

"I don't know," I said, "let's get going."

Roy made the giant cracks in the ground disappear by making pillars of rock so we could walk right over the cracks. We took a while getting out of the cave, bu not nearly as long as it had taken us to get where we were. I saw that four of us had our orbs, and Lauren was that only one left. I felt kind of bad for her, but knowing her, she would probably be fine. I wished we could just go find her orb and get the whole thing over with, but we still had to get her map from Eve. We finally got out of the cave, and there was real sunlight again.

"Hey," said Roy, "I'm going to put my orb into my sword now. Let's see what happens." he put the orb into it's place and the sword turned to stone, "Are you kidding me?" he shouted, "I thought mine would be something cooler!"

"Hey," said Xavier, "I wouldn't be complaining if I were you; my bow didn't do anything!"

"Calm down," Lauren said, "we have something more important to do."

"And what would that be?" asked Roy.

"I still need my orb."

WE BATTLE A CRAZY MONKEY

Rick

As we walked into Aric's house, I remembered how long ago it had been since Eve had given us the maps. I realized how anxious Lauren must have been and how long she must have been waiting. We walked into the room that we had all been talking in, and I saw Aric and Eve sitting next to each other on the couch. They were in about the same place they were in when we had left a few days before. They were talking about something or the other, but they stopped as soon as they saw us walk in.

"Did you find them all?" asked Eve.

Chapter Eighteen

"Yeah, so can you give us the map now?" asked Roy, "Because this is seriously taking forever."

"It just seems like that," said Lauren, "but it's only been a few days."

"Lauren's right," said Aric, "you did find those orbs pretty fast. I thought I had protected them pretty well."

"So will you give us the map now?" Roy said to Eve.

"Well, my dad convinced me that you guys are doing the right thing, so I guess I will, but I didn't bring the map with me, so we'll have to go back to my house to get it," she replied. *I really wish we don't have to do this,* I thought, *I think we've walked our fair share in the last few days.*

"Do we all have to go?" complained Roy.

"Not if you don't want to, but didn't you say it's dangerous for me to be out here by myself?"

"I think someone other than me should go with Eve in case of an attack," said Lauren.

"I'll go," said Alex. Eve and Alex walked out of the house and back to her house to get the map. I was thankful that I didn't have to go so I could get some rest.

"What do we do now?" asked Roy.

We Battle a Crazy Monkey

"We wait," said Xavier as he sat down on the couch across from where Aric was sitting. I saw that it was a good idea, and I sat down too.

"How did you find the orbs so fast?" asked Aric.

"I think it's just because Lauren's so good at figuring things out," I said.

"And I'm not?" asked Xavier.

"I just mean that Lauren solved the riddle," I said. After that, we all just sat around, thinking about our own things and waiting for Alex and Eve to come back. We waited and waited until they finally burst through the door.

"We got it," Alex announced.

"Took you long enough!" said Roy.

"Did anything happen to you?" I asked.

"Nope, everything was perfectly fine," said Alex with a grin on her face.

Eve handed the last map to Lauren and said, "Here you go."

"Thank you," he replied.

Chapter Eighteen

"Are we going to go now?" asked Roy. He was either really anxious to find all the orbs, or he was just bored and he wanted something to do.

"Right after I figure out where we have to go," said Lauren.

"Oh, right," said Roy. It only took Lauren a few moments to figure out where we had to go, and we set off after that. I felt like we were nomads because we had been traveling so often lately.

"So where do we have to go exactly?" asked Alex.

"We have to go to what looks like a jungle on the map somewhere not far from here," said Lauren. She led us out of Aric's house and in the opposite direction that the mountain range was in. We walked behind Lauren as she looked at her map every so often to check that we were going in the right direction. After a while, I could start to see trees on the horizon, and I could easily tell that it was the beginning of a forest.

"There it is," said Lauren.

"How much longer until we get there?" asked Roy.

We Battle a Crazy Monkey

"I don't know," I said, "I don't think it's possible to estimate walking distances without knowing how far we have to go."

Roy kept complaining about how we had to walk so much and other things, but I just started to ignore him. He's not usually annoying; he just has a lot to complain about. If he was annoying, he wouldn't be my friend.

Anyways, we got to the forest about four or five hours after we had left from Aric's house, but we were hungry. The trees in front of the forest were about fifteen to twenty feet tall at the most, and the ground became completely grassy. It was starting to get dark outside; it was probably about five in the afternoon. Roy found a banana tree, and he made a pillar of earth under himself so he could reach the bananas. We devoured them in minutes like we were monkeys.

"I never thought I'd be so happy to eat a banana," said Alex.

"Same here," I said. I had never like bananas, but after you haven't eaten in about a day, you tend to eat anything edible.

"Where do we go now?" asked Xavier.

Chapter Eighteen

"Into the forest; the orb should be at about the center of the forest, if Aric's map is accurate," said Lauren after she had just finished her last banana.

"We still have more walking to do?" complained Roy.

"At least it's not on an empty stomach," I said.

"Let's go," said Lauren. He led us into the jungle, and it was dark because of the canopy of trees above us. I had read about jungles when I was a little kid, and had seen pictures too, but it was nothing compared to the real thing. I'm not entirely sure I can explain it to you completely, but I'll try.

There were trees all around us; everything was green. There were flowers of all sorts of colors coming out of the ground which was completely covered with grass. There were monkeys going from tree to tree and birds flying around, and their chirping was calming. I could barely see more than fifteen feet in front of me because there were trees in the way of my vision. As we walked along, I saw vines hanging down from trees, and there was a snake hanging from a tree, but I mistook it for a vine. It scared the heck out of me when it started hissing.

"How long until we get to the middle?" asked Roy.

We Battle a Crazy Monkey

"I don't know, but if we keep going straight, we're bound to get to the center sometime," said Lauren. She looked at her map again and we kept going. I was starting to understand why Roy wanted to get to the middle so fast. It was getting tiring and boring; we were just walking and walking. After a while, I could see a dark figure behind the trees, and I was wondering what it was.

"We're almost at the center," said Lauren while looking down at her map. We reached the center of the forest, and I could tell what the dark figure was. We all stopped and looked at it in wonder, but Lauren was still looking at the map.

"Why did everyone stop?" she asked, confused. Xavier turned her head up so she could see in front of her, "Oh," she said.

"I think someone beat us here," said Roy.

"Thank you captain obvious," said Xavier.

"You're welcome, lieutenant sarcasm," said Roy with a smile on his face. I smiled, and I held back a laugh because Xavier looked annoyed.

I looked at the large stone fort in wonder, "Do we go in, or what?" I asked.

Chapter Eighteen

"I think that's the only thing to do," said Xavier.

We walked toward the stone archway that led to the inside. It was about ten feet tall, but the entire place looked about twenty feet tall. It was big, but it was nothing compared to the wolves' castle. When we stepped in, I heard sounds of monkeys coming from all around. I couldn't see any monkeys, but it was pretty obvious that they were around. The biggest clue was that there were banana peels all over the ground. The ground was still made of dirt though.

"I'm not the only one that hears monkey sounds, right?" Roy whispered.

"Nope, I hear them too," I whispered back.

"Okay, good."

Out of nowhere, monkeys dropped from the walls and started attacking us (that is the *weirdest* sentence I have ever heard).

"What do we do now?" asked Alex.

"We attack!" I said as a monkey jumped onto me. I pushed it away and took out my sword on instinct. It was the first time I would get to try my new powers, and it was great that we all had our orbs. Even though Lauren didn't have hers, at least she had her bow and she was stocked with arrows.

"Lauren! I need some arrows!" shouted Xavier right after he whacked a monkey like a baseball with his bow. Lauren ran over to him and handed him a few arrows from her quiver. Meanwhile, Alex's sword made of fire was actually solid; so it could hit monkeys, but they'd catch on fire. It was a strange sight to see. Flaming monkeys were running around and screaming. Normally I would not like to kill animals but this time it was a question of life or death. (Disclaimer: Whatever harm we did to the monkeys was purely for self defense.)

Roy was taking stones from the top of the fort and started hurling them at any monkey that tried to attack him. I pushed my hand forward and a stream of air shot forward at a monkey, flinging it back to the wall. "Whoa," I said. I hadn't known what I could do.

Xavier shot an arrow at a monkey, and right before it hit, a wave exploded out of the arrow and the monkey was nowhere to be seen afterward. "I was wrong," he said, "my weapon is the coolest."

Chapter Eighteen

The battle raged on and on and on. Xavier and Lauren were aiming their last arrows when the monkeys stopped attacking. They all stood in place staring at something in the other direction. I held my sword at my side and turned around. There was a hallway leading into the room we were in, and I could hear feet pounding on the ground as something approached. There was a large shadow on the wall that looked huge. *If that's only the shadow,* I thought, *then how big is the real thing?*

"I hope this doesn't turn into one of the stories where the bad guys win," said Roy.

"That never happens," whispered Xavier.

"Hopefully," muttered Roy.

When the shadow was almost gone, I could see the figure. It was another monkey, but it was bigger. Judging by its size, it was probably the king. The most obvious reason was that he was wearing a crown. I didn't know what to do, and I didn't want to bow down to him like the other monkeys were. All five of us got in a small bunch and Roy started talking somewhat loudly.

"Who's that guy?" asked Roy.

We Battle a Crazy Monkey

Just then, the monkey was in front of us and he said, "I think the better question is, who are *you*?" He started laughing loudly like maniac. He talked somewhat slow; compared to how most people would talk. He also stood on his hands rather than his feet, and he would randomly turn upside down with his feet in the air while he was talking. Sometimes he would even stand on one hand and jump in the air and land on his feet.

"We're humans from a different world," I said truthfully.

"That's crazy, man," he said while his head bobbled around, "I'm the king of this place, my name is King Rumel."

I turned back to Roy, Xavier, Alex and Lauren and said, "I think we should just ask this guy where the orb is."

"This guy has the orb, of course," he said as he walked around us on his hands.

"Can you give it to us?" I asked hopefully.

"That's an idea," he said, "but it's mine." King Rumel ran to the right wall on his feet and jumped up about ten feet in the air. He grabbed onto a rock and started climbing up. My eyes widened when I saw that. When he got to the top, he sat on the wall.

"Well we need it," I said.

"I bet you do," he replied. He started laughing again. *What's his problem?* Then he started talking again, "I'll make you a deal."

"What is it?" asked Roy.

"Whoa, slow down there. I'll tell you. If you can knock me down in a battle, you can take the round thing." He then jumped off the wall and landed on his feet. He immediately started walking on his hands again and he walked over to us.

"Sure, let's go," I said.

"Only one at a time," he said, "I can't handle all five of you," he then started laughing again.

"Who wants to go first?" I asked.

"I will!" said Roy enthusiastically.

The monkeys we had been fighting earlier had all spread out along the walls of the fort, leaving the place open for King Rumel and Roy to fight. It wasn't my first choice of methods to get the orb, but I didn't think we could get the orb any other way. We all stepped back towards the wall to give them more room, and Roy took out his sword.

"Did I say anything about weapons?" he asked. Roy put his sword away, "I didn't think so!" King Rumel started laughing loudly again. I think he was too sure that nobody could knock him down.

"What are you waiting for?" asked the monkey.

Just then, Roy took a rock from the top of the fort using his powers from the orb and flung it at King Rumel. The King ducked under it and it crashed into the wall. He was laughing again, but this time he was laughing at Roy. Roy seemed angry; like he would always be if someone made fun of him.

He brought a rock down from behind the laughing monkey, and pulled it towards him. Instinctively, the monkey jumped up from his legs and perfectly landed on the stone heading straight towards Roy. He barely stopped the stone about one foot from his face and the monkey jumped off.

"Do you give up yet?"

"Nope," responded Roy. He started getting mad and throwing rocks from anywhere and everywhere at the king, but he kept jumping out of the way. I could tell Roy was getting frustrated, and King Rumel just kept laughing and laughing. Roy threw a rock backward, and it hit the wall a few inches to my right.

"Roy!" I shouted, "I think you should let someone else try now!"

Roy stopped his rock in midair, put it back from where it came from and walked to the wall where we were standing. His face was completely red and he was breathing hard.

"You okay?" I asked.

"Yeah," he responded while still panting.

"I'll go," I said.

I stepped forward and the monkey said, "So now it's your turn!" he immediately started laughing. I tried to catch him off guard by shooting a stream of air directly at him. Apparently I did, but I hit him square in the chest so all that happened was he got slammed into the wall. I thought I had won, but I remembered that the deal was to knock him down.

"Yeah, go Rick!" shouted Alex.

We Battle a Crazy Monkey

For the first time, King Rumel wasn't laughing. I realized that I had to hit him in a different place. I knew his feet would be the best target, but his feet were rarely on the ground. He was either on his hands, or jumping in the air. It wasn't the easiest way to go, but it was the only plan I had.

I shot another stream of air at him, but that time, he was expecting it, so he moved out the way fast. I ran towards him so I would have a better shot at hitting him, but at the same time, he ran to the other wall. He started climbing up the wall; only making it harder for me. I shot streams of air at him, but I kept hitting the rocks. He finally got to the top and he sat there, mocking me because I couldn't hit him.

King Rumel started walking around the perimeter of the fort. I started to get frustrated because he would move before I was able to hit him. I started shooting air at him rapidly, almost like a machine gun, but he would always do some crazy move to dodge them, like standing on one hand upside down and jumping up. Or he would just jump ten feet in the air.

Chapter Eighteen

This guy is insane! I thought, *there's no way I can beat him!* Just then, I remembered Aric's story. I tried to create a tornado, but apparently it would take a lot of practice because I could barely swirl the air enough to pick up a few banana peels.

King Rumel looked like he was getting bored waiting for me to attack him. He jumped down from the fort's wall and did stunts while he was waiting. I finally got so tired of not being able to hit him that I decided to run up to him so I would have a guaranteed shot at him.

I sprinted as hard as I could so the monkey king wouldn't have much time to run away. When I was a few feet away, I slipped on a banana peel and crashed into King Rumel.

Not exactly what I had in mind, but that works too.

"You did it!" shouted Alex.

I got up off of King Rumel and he got up after me. He was on his hands and he held out his foot. I shook his foot and he said, "Good job."

"Do I get the orb now?" I asked.

"The what?" he asked jokingly.

"The orb," I repeated.

We Battle a Crazy Monkey

"You must mean that round thing I found," he said as he flipped himself upside down.

"Yeah, that thing," I said.

"Yeknom," he called. I thought he had officially gone insane (I'm not implying that he's *not* insane, don't get me wrong) until another monkey answered him.

"Yes sir," said another monkey as it approached King Rumel.

"Get me the round shiny thing we found will you?"

"Yes sir," the monkey replied. It ran to the hallway that King Rumel had come out of on its knuckles and feet. A few minutes later, the monkey (whose name was apparently Yeknom) came out holding the orb in its left hand. It handed the orb to King Rumel, and he took it in his right foot.

"Can I have it now?" I asked.

"Can you?" he asked. Then he started laughing.

"Can you *give* it to me?" I asked.

"I can," he replied.

"Fine, *may* you give me the orb?!" I asked.

"Yes I may! Under one condition: you give it back to me every winter." he said.

"Okay," I said. He handed me the orb (with his foot) and Lauren walked over to get it from me.

"You got it for me," she said.

"Yes I did," I replied.

"Can I see it?" she asked.

"What does it look like?" I asked. I guess King Rumel had rubbed off on me, "I'm just kidding, here you go," I gave the orb to Lauren. She stared at it in amazement and held it in her hands like it was her most prized possession. The orb was clear, but there were plants growing around the inside of it.

"Put it in your bow," I said. She did what I said, but nothing happened.

"Maybe it's like Xavier's," he said, "I think something will only happen once I shoot an arrow at something."

"Let's hope so," I said. I thought for a while, and I eventually came to a question, "Hey King Rumel, how did you get the orb in the first place?"

"Well, last winter, all of the trees stopped growing fruits, and we were starving. We went out looking for food and we came to this very spot, and the trees were growing like crazy. I wanted to know why that stuff was growing, so we dug up that spot. We found that shiny orb and we found out later that it helps plants grow. That's why we built our fort here."

"Nice story," I said, "but I have one last favor to ask you. Will you help us take back the wolves' kingdom?"

"Well, what's in it for me?" he asked.

"We'll..." I thought for a moment; *what could he want?* "We'll help you expand your kingdom," I suggested.

"I can do that myself," he said, "what else you got?"

"Wait, since we won the battle, shouldn't we get the orb free of charge?" I asked.

"Fine," said King Rumel.

"Then what you get in return for helping us is the orb back every winter," I said.

"All right," he said, but he sounded disappointed.

MONKEY POWER!

Rick

"The only way they won't notice us is if we sneak in at night," I said.

"But how do we know if we'll get there at night?" asked Xavier, "Because if we leave at night, then we won't even get there until midday."

"Then we leave during the day, and wait about an hour's walk away until it's night," I said. I was proud of myself; I had made a plan that might actually work, "then, we attack."

"So should we leave now?" asked Xavier, "It's daytime right now, and the earlier we leave, the better."

Monkey Power!

"Sounds great to me!" said King Rumel while he was standing on his left hand.

"How fast can you get your army ready?" I asked him.

"They can be ready in minutes," he said while jumping off of his hand and landing on his feet.

"Can they be ready in thirty minutes?" I asked.

"Can they?"

"May you get them ready in thirty minutes?" I asked, somewhat annoyed.

"Yes I may," he responded as he walked away.

"All right," I said to my four friends, "we have all of thirty minutes. Is everyone ready?"

"Lauren and I have only one arrow left," said Xavier.

"What can we do about that?" I asked.

"We can cut down a tree from outside so we can get some wood," suggested Lauren.

"And I can make some arrowheads out of stone," said Roy.

"Great, so get to it," I said, "we only have thirty minutes to make as many arrows as you guys might need."

Chapter Nineteen

Lauren walked around and she found the perfect tree. It was right next to the archway that we had come in from. The tree was about six feet tall, but Lauren said she needed more wood; so she decided to make it grow. A ball of pure energy formed in Lauren's hands and the energy flowed down to the tree, and it started growing like anything.

"Wow," I said. I had never seen anything like it. It was like watching a plant grow in fast-forward. A few seconds later, the tree was taller than I was and the ball of energy in Lauren's hands was almost gone. The energy stopped flowing to the tree, and Lauren opened her eyes.

"That took a lot less time and energy than before," said Lauren, "I guess the orb really does help a lot."

"Roy, did you make any arrowheads yet?" I asked.

He was sitting a few feet away from us, and he was sharpening a rock with his sword, "You gave me two minutes! I only have one done so far!"

"Okay, great job," I said.

"How are we supposed to get any wood from this?" asked Alex.

"We cut it down," replied Lauren.

"And how are you planning to do that?" asked Xavier.

"I don't know," said Lauren.

"I can try to cut it down with my sword," I suggested. I took out my sword and swung it at the tree. My sword hit the trunk and only made about a one inch cut.

"Let me try," said Alex. She took out her sword, but noticed that it was on fire, "on second thought, I probably don't want to burn down this tree," she put away her sword and I gave her mine to use. She tried to hold it, but she couldn't grab the hilt. I guess I was the only one that could hold the tornado. I popped the orb out of the bottom and the hilt turned normal again. She swung at it in the same place, and he did no better than me.

"Hey Roy," I called, "can you try?"

"More work?" he complained.

"Hey, you volunteered to help with the arrowheads," I pointed out.

"Fine," he said. He came over to where we were, and he took out his sword. He took a swing at it, and his sword cut through it like butter.

"Are you really that much stronger than us?" asked Alex.

"I don't think so," he said, "it was actually pretty easy."

"Easy? I put all of my strength into my swing, and it barely went an inch deep!" I said.

"Maybe it's his sword," suggested Lauren.

"Let me see that," said Alex. She took Roy's sword and cut the tree's trunk in half straight down the middle, "it's definitely the sword."

"Can we use your sword?" I asked, "You can use mine."

"Fine, take it," he said.

"Great," I said right before I pulled out my sword and handed it to him, "here you go."

He took my sword and went back to what he was doing. I used his sword to cut the tree into small pieces and Lauren rounded them off after I was done. We took some of the arrowhead that Roy had made and put them on the ends of the sticks. By the time we were done, King Rumel had just gotten his army together; it was perfect timing. He walked out of the hallway with all of his monkeys behind him, and none of them had weapons.

Monkey Power!

Apparently monkeys can fight really well, and that had been proven when we were fighting them earlier.

"Do both of you have enough arrows now?" I asked.

"Yeah, I think fifteen each is enough," responded Xavier.

"Hey King Rumel," I said, "Are you ready to leave?" I asked.

"I think we should leave tomorrow. It would give everyone more time to rest and prepare," said the monkey king. That was about the first intelligent comment he had made since we met him.

"Okay," I said. We stayed there for the rest of the day, and slept when it got dark. I woke up and we left almost right away.

"Let's go," I said. We walked out of the fort and we started our journey back to the castle. I bet that you're probably tired of hearing about us walking around all day, so I'll skip all the unimportant minor details and just summarize it for you.

"Why can't we just ride animals, like horses or something?" asked Roy, "That would make our lives so much easier."

Chapter Nineteen

"Do you see any horses around here?" I asked him in return.

"No, but I still wish we had some."

"If I could find some better form of transportation, we would be using it, but there isn't. So you'll just have to deal with us walking everywhere."

We walked on and on with Lauren leading the way since she could read maps the best. The monkeys had picked some bananas from trees on the way, and we did the same. Roy was obviously complaining the whole way, as usual. King Rumel didn't seem to get tired at all, no matter what happened. Once we got out of the forest, there was still a long way to go. The trip took an entire day longer than we had expected. We had camped out an hour away from the castle, but we were there a day later than we had expected.

"What do we do now?" asked Roy.

"We have to wait until sundown," said Xavier, "then we sneak in."

"What are we going to do until then?" asked Alex.

"Didn't I just say that?" asked Xavier, "We wait!"

Monkey Power!

And so we waited, and waited. It took a long while, but sundown eventually came. We walked to the castle for an hour, and by that time, we had the dark cloak of night concealing us from our enemies.

"When do we go?" asked Roy.

"Now!" I whispered. We ran to the front of the castle, and there were about twenty foxes standing guard. They had apparently been awake because I could hear them snarling at us. Roy took a rock from the ground and hit as many of them on the head as he could; knocking them out. Xavier fired an arrow and a wave of water exploded on two of the foxes, and I couldn't tell what happened to them. Lauren shot an arrow at the last fox, and when it hit its target, vines started growing out of the arrow and wrapping around the fox. It was covered in plants, and it had probably been suffocated.

"So that's what my orb does," whispered Lauren.

We ran inside the castle and we woke up the foxes. They were no match for the monkeys. They would hide by hanging onto the rocks on the walls of the castle and then start attacking. Most people might call it cowardly fighting, but I called it brilliant.

Chapter Nineteen

"We have to find Bailey!" I shouted. I could barely hear myself over the snarling of the foxes and the screeching of the monkeys.

"Well where would he be?" asked Xavier.

"I'm guessing he'll be in the king's room!" I shouted.

"Then let's go!" shouted Xavier. We ran to the king's room and there were at least fifty foxes waiting for us.

"How are we supposed to do this?" asked Alex.

"I don't know!" I shouted, "Just do the best you can!"

"Okay!"

I blew back some foxes with streams of air, but it wasn't good enough. I took out my sword and started furiously slashing at any fox that got in my way. Alex was doing the same thing, except that any fox that got in her way would get slashed and burned. Lauren and Xavier couldn't do much more than shoot arrows at foxes, until they found out how to use their element. After Xavier shot an arrow, he would use the water that exploded out of it, and Lauren would make the plants grow bigger so they could strangle more than one fox at a time. Roy was taking rocks from out of the ground and throwing them at the foxes. The entire castle was made of stone, including the ground, so it made it a lot easier for Roy.

It seemed like we were about to lose, but then I heard some monkeys running towards us. They jumped on the remaining foxes and pounded them to the ground. The foxes had obviously been outnumbered.

At one point, I wasn't paying attention to everything around me, so a fox got to me and scratched my left leg badly. I screamed for a second, but I got over it so I could keep on fighting.

"You okay?" asked Lauren.

I gave her a weak thumbs up and said, "I'm fine."

I tried walking around, but I realized that I had a limp, so I fought in one place. Eventually, there were no more foxes left to fight; mostly because the monkeys had saved us. I opened the door to the king's room and saw Bailey sitting on King Olkin's chair. I had thought we had finally gotten to him, but I saw more foxes waiting for us. This time, there were about seventy all lined up and ready to fight, but we were already tired from the foxes we had just fought.

Chapter Nineteen

"How did you get in here?" asked Bailey, "No matter, you won't last for very long. Attack!" the foxes charged us and I knew that there was no way I would be able to fight more than five foxes. Just when they were about to reach us, Alex created a wall of fire in front of us so the foxes couldn't get through. The fire was in a straight line from one side of the room to the other, keeping the foxes out. Meanwhile, the monkeys started climbing on the wall to get over the fire and jumping to the other side. Almost all of the monkeys went to the other side, and that really helped us.

"Nice job," said Xavier, "but what now?"

"I don't know! I don't usually think that far ahead! I was just trying to keep us alive!" shouted Alex. By that time, I was on the ground looking at my leg because it really hurt. There were three claw marks running down the side of my leg and they were about a foot long. It wasn't that deep, but it stung. It had turned the bottom of my pants red, and there was still blood coming.

"That looks bad," said Roy.

"Well can someone help me?" I asked.

"I still have some water from when I last shot an arrow," said Xavier, "maybe that will help."

"Yes it will," I said, "so can you put it on?" Xavier lifted the ball of water that he had without touching it, and poured some of it onto my wound. It stung at first, but it felt better after a little bit. Once there was no more water left, Xavier ripped off the bottom of my pants to use as cloth around my wound. He threw away the side that had come from my left leg, and used the cloth from my right leg to wrap around my wound.

I slowly got up, and my leg was feeling a whole lot better than before. At least I could walk around. I looked at Alex's wall of fire, and through it, I saw the foxes waiting for it to go away so they could attack us.

"Let's roll," I said. With that, we all readied our weapons and Alex calmed the fire down until it was completely gone. The foxes charged at us, and Lauren wrapped as many foxes as she could in plants at once. He got about half of the ones that weren't already being attacked by monkeys, and they got strangled by the vines. *Thank you, Lauren,* I thought.

Chapter Nineteen

I pushed a bunch of the foxes to the wall, and I kept pushing them against the wall until they were knocked out. Roy, Xavier and Alex took care of the rest of the foxes. We had beaten them a lot faster than I had expected, and we owed it all to the monkeys.

I looked up at Bailey, and he was staring at us in amazement. Apparently he had underestimated how good we were. He had probably thought we wouldn't even get past the foxes that we had battled outside.

"Now I get to personally destroy all of you," he said. He shot lightning out of his fingertips at all of us, and we all moved out of the way less than half a second before they would have hit us. The lightning exploded the ground on impact. There was a bunch of dust that got stirred up, and when it all cleared, Bailey was gone.

"There's only one place he could have gone!" I said, "Outside the castle!" we sprinted out of the castle so that we could catch up with him, but we weren't fast enough. Once we were outside, I saw him running in the direction of the forest that the portal was in.

"Let's go!" shouted Xavier. We all ran after him and I was sprinting as fast as I could. I would have gone faster, but my leg was slowing me down. Luckily, my right leg was my dominant leg, so I wasn't being slowed down as much as I could have been. He was too far ahead of us for us to catch him, so I told Xavier and Lauren to try and shoot him. They both missed because it was hard to aim while running. Eventually, we followed Bailey all the way to the portal. *What's he doing?* I wondered, *Is he going to go into our world?* My question was answered when he shot a bolt of lightning at the bush when he was about fifty feet away from it. It caught on fire, and all I could do was watch.

"Alex! Can you stop the fire?" I asked.

"I already tried! It's too far away for me to control it!" she responded. By the time we were close enough to do anything about the fire, the bush was completely burned up.

"What did you do!?" I screamed at him.

"Isn't it obvious?" he asked with a small grin on his face, "I destroyed the portal."

I got extremely mad, and I was about to blow him away. I saw that he was making a ball of lightning in his hands and he was probably going to shoot it all at me.

Chapter Nineteen

Suddenly, there was a cloud of dust around me and the ground beneath me was gone. I landed on my bottom about seven feet below the surface. Then, the space above got closed off by rocks. My first thought was, *Is this an ambush?* It was pitch black, but heard my friends' voices, so at least I knew they were there too.

"What happened?" I heard Alex ask.

"It's okay," said Roy, "I did this."

"Why?" I asked.

"So Bailey wouldn't kill us all!" he responded.

"Hey Alex," I said, "Would you mind making a small fire in your hands so we can all see?"

"No problem," he said. Almost immediately, there was light and I could see where we were. Roy had made a trench and sealed it off so Bailey couldn't kill us. It was about ten feet wide and twenty feet long. I could see Lauren, Alex, Xavier and Roy all standing behind me.

"What do we do now?" I asked.

"I think that's the whole reason behind us being here," said Xavier, "we don't have a plan to beat Bailey."

"Yeah we do!" I said.

"What? Are we just going to go up to him and try to knock him out when he's free to shoot lightning at any one of us and kill us? We need a better plan than that."

"You're right," I said.

"So what's our new plan?" asked Roy.

"Well, I think the only way he won't be able to shoot lightning at us is if he's tied up, right?" I asked.

"So we're just going to go up to him without any rope or chains, and try to tie him up?" asked Xavier. He was probably confused at what I was trying to get at.

"No, Lauren can tie him up with some plants," I said.

"Okay, then what?" asked Xavier.

"Well, there was something that Aric told me about, and he said it took out an entire army of foxes at once," I said; remembering his story.

"What is it?" asked Roy impatiently.

I told them what Aric had told me, but in the shortest way possible. I wanted to get back up there as soon as possible.

"All right," said Lauren, "but can you really make a tornado?"

"I hope so," I said.

Chapter Nineteen

"That's not good enough!" said Xavier, "We need to be sure that our plan will work, or else we might literally die!"

"Okay, I'll try to make a small one here," I said. They all backed away to the opposite end of the trench that I was on. I tried swirling the air in a circle, but it never worked, just like when I had tried it before on the monkeys. I got frustrated, but I told myself to calm down and keep trying. It wasn't working, so I started to think again like I usually do. At one point in my thoughts, my sword came to mind, and I suddenly remembered how it looked once I put my orb in.

I stopped trying to swirl the air, and I took out my sword. I saw the hilt turn into a tornado, and I saw the small tornado on the tip of the blade. I knew that I could use it to my advantage, so I did. I made the tornado grow bigger, and I took it off of the tip of my sword. I put my sword away, and I made the tornado grow bigger until it was about three feet tall and was collecting a lot of dirt. I stopped it because I had proved to everyone that I could create a tornado.

"Okay, now I'm officially convinced that this plan will work," said Xavier confidently.

"Everyone knows what to do?" I asked. Everyone nodded yes.

"Are we ready to fight?" asked Roy.

"One second," I said. I calmed myself down, and I made sure that I wasn't nervous, "Okay, now I'm ready."

Roy took away the cover to the trench and raised the ground to normal level. Lauren had her bow ready, so she shot an arrow at Bailey, who was facing us about fifteen feet away. He had just enough time to save himself; he quickly shot a bolt of lightning at the arrow and it exploded into bark. He started laughing evilly and said, "Is that the best you've got?"

I looked at Xavier, and he looked really ticked off. He strung an arrow and shot at Bailey. Just before Bailey was going to shoot lightning at it, the arrow exploded into a wave. Lauren had just enough time to shoot an arrow at him without it being blown to bits.

The arrow hit its mark, and plants started growing out of it. Bailey apparently had some armor underneath his clothing because there was no blood. Vines wrapped around his body, and grew into the ground; making sure that he was immobilized. Right after he was completely still, Roy made a wall of earth about ten feet in diameter around him. I made a tornado the same way I had in the trench, but I made it a lot bigger. We all ran back about twenty feet because none of us wanted to be picked up by the tornado.

"Now add some water!" I shouted at Xavier over the roar of wind.

"How?!"

"I don't know! Try shooting an arrow at it!"

He strung his last arrow and shot it at the tornado. The wave that exploded out of it became an entire layer of water; making it a hurricane.

"Roy!" I shouted. He gave me a thumbs up and let down part of the wall that was directly in front of Bailey. Alex lit him on fire, and we let the hurricane loose. When it got close to where Bailey was standing, the wall of earth crumbled and started swirling in the hurricane. Bailey was still planted firmly on the ground because the vines had grown into the ground. The hurricane hit him, and I was blinded by all of the dust that was stirred up.

Monkey Power!

When the dust cleared, all I could see was a body lying on the ground. It was a pretty gory scene. He was lying on the ground with his clothes ripped and bloody, and there was blood still coming. I kind of felt sorry for the guy, but I knew it was what we had to do.

"Serves him right," said Roy.

"What do we do now?" asked Alex.

"We take him back and lock him up," I said. Lauren and Roy picked him up and took him back to the castle. When we got there, I asked, "Does anyone know if there's a jail cell anywhere?"

"Oh, I do," said Alex. She took us to the end of the hallway that led to the king's room and he opened a trap door on the floor. I had noticed that there was one thing about the castle that looked different. The walls weren't a dark shade of black anymore, they were actually a shade of maroon. I had never known that the castle could look like that.

Alex made a fire in front of us and we walked down the small slope. When we got there, I saw that on both sides of the seemingly endless hall were jail cells. The weird thing was that they were all full. There were all sorts of animals down there; I was guessing that when Bailey had taken over the castle, he had locked all of them down there.

"We have to get all of these guys out of here!" I exclaimed. We all went down the hallway opening the sliding bars and letting out all of the animals.

Every time I would open a cell, I would hear a "Thank you." It felt nice to be appreciated. Once we were done, we still had to put Bailey in a cell.

"Let's put him in the one at the end of the hall," suggested Roy.

"Sure," I said.

"Wait," said Xavier, "Once he wakes up, won't he be able to bust himself out again?"

"You're right," I said. I took his sword from his side (still in its sheath so it wouldn't shock me) and put it in the cell on the opposite side of the hall in the first cell. I made sure that it would be so far away that he couldn't control lightning anymore.

"Great idea," said Lauren when I got back.

"Just to make sure he doesn't escape," said Roy, "I'll make a wall." I wasn't sure what he meant at first, but then, he made a wall of earth as tall as the ceiling right in front of the cell with a hole at eye level so he could breathe.

"Nice work," said Xavier.

"Thank you," responded Roy, also seeming pleased with what he had done. When we were about to leave the dungeon, Roy made a wall of earth in front of the cell that was holding his sword, too. I thought that we were finally finished with what we had to do, until I remembered the most important thing that we had left. We still had to rescue King Olkin.

WE MEET THE KING

Rick

We got to Aric's house a few hours after we had left. I knocked on the door, it swung open a few moments later, and I saw Eve standing in the doorway, "Where were you guys?! You took so long to come back, I thought something horrible had happened!" she screamed at us the second she saw us. What a warm welcome.

"Let them come in first," said Aric from behind her. Eve immediately stepped aside and we walked in. we all sat down in our usual seats; Aric's house was beginning to feel like a home.

"So, I'm curious too, what *did* happen?" asked Aric.

We Meet the King

"Well, to make a long story short, after we got Lauren's orb, we got the help of the monkeys to take the wolves' kingdom back," I started.

"Wait, where did the monkeys come from?" asked Eve confusedly.

"There was this crazy monkey king that had the orb, so we fought him for it, and after that, we became friends and they helped us win back the castle," said Alex.

"Okay, then what happened?" Eve asked.

"Well, we beat up Bailey, the guy who can control lightning, we put him in jail, and now we're here," said Roy.

"And why are you here?" asked Aric.

"We would have gone directly to the foxes' castle, except that we have absolutely no idea how to get there." I said.

"Is that the only reason you're here?" asked Eve, "Because you wanted directions?"

"Yeah, pretty much," I said. Eve stormed off into the hallway, muttering something about me.

"Did I do something?" I asked.

Chapter Twenty

"Don't worry," said Aric, "she can be a bit moody sometimes."

"Okay," I said, still kind of confused.

"You said you need directions to the foxes' castle?" asked Aric.

"Yeah," I said.

"I think I can help you there," he said, "I've been there before."

"Great," I said, "can you give us directions?"

"It's hard to explain, so I'll draw you a map," he said, "do any of you have paper?"

"You can use the back of my map," said Lauren.

"Perfect," said Aric while taking a pencil out from his pocket. He put the map on the table, and started drawing. About five minutes later, there was a full map of the area and a path that lead directly to the foxes' castle. It was designed like a treasure map; there was a circle at where we were and an X at where the castle was.

"About how long do you think this might take?" I asked.

"At most, it would probably take about a day or so."

"Sounds good," I said.

We Meet the King

"When do we leave?" asked Lauren.

"The sooner the better," I said, "so now, I guess." We all got up, thanked Aric, and left. I was sick of walking, and hopefully it would be the last time we would have to for a while, but knowing my luck; it wouldn't be. We actually got there the next morning, like I had hoped.

Once we were there, Xavier asked a very reasonable question, "How are we going to do this exactly? Because I really don't want to fight any more foxes."

"I know where King Olkin is being held, so finding him shouldn't be that hard, as for avoiding a fight in enemy territory, that might be more of a challenge," I said.

"So what can we do?' asked Alex.

"I have no idea," I said, "how about you, Lauren?"

"We can always try just sneaking past anyone there," he suggested.

"That's pretty risky; what if someone sees us?" asked Xavier.

"Then we have to fight, but does anyone have a better plan?" I said, looking around, "No? Then I guess we'll go with Lauren's idea."

Chapter Twenty

I walked up to the front of the castle, and I noticed that it actually looked kind of like the wolves' castle, except a lot more depressing. The walls were a shade of gray, and it looked like the regular color. It looked like the stereotypical evil person's castle; all it needed were some dark clouds and some lightning. There were two foxes standing guard, and they looked bigger than normal foxes. They would walk back and forth, going from opposite sides of the castle back to the middle; where the door was.

We were actually hiding behind the archway that led to the door, and the guards were standing directly in front of the door. The archway was huge; about fifty feet tall, and the pillars were about five feet wide, so we could all hide behind them without being seen.

"How are we supposed to get out of this one without fighting?" whispered Roy.

"I have no idea," I whispered back.

"Hey wait," said Lauren, "What if we sneak in while they're facing the other way?"

"Great idea," I responded.

We Meet the King

"We have to go one at a time, and the first person will keep the door open for the rest of us," said Lauren.

"I'll go first," volunteered Xavier. He ran forward while the guards were facing the other direction, opened the door and barely got inside. The guards turned around just as soon as Xavier closed the door. Next, Alex ran through and Xavier opened the door for her. Then went Lauren, Roy, and I was last. I crept forward so that they wouldn't hear me. I felt like I was in some kids' video game. I got inside, and shut the door behind me. *Yes!* I thought, *We didn't have to fight anything this time!*

"Is there anyone around?" I whispered just after we got inside. Roy pushed the door to make sure that it was completely closed. The floor was made of stone, just like in the wolves' castle, but the rest looked completely different. The inside of the castle looked like a giant, dark hallway.

Probably on instinct, Alex made a small fire in her hand again so we could see. She kept the flame small, so nobody would notice us, "No," she whispered back.

On the floors, there were skeletons of many dead animals. I could hear creepy noises coming from anywhere and everywhere in the castle. I had to gather all of my courage to take one step. If I had a choice, I would have run out of there as soon as possible.

We finally got to the end of the hall, and just like the fox had said, there was a spiraling staircase. The stairs looked wooden, and there were no handrails, so if you fell, you died. All you could do was put your hand on the wall for balance. There were cobwebs everywhere and the place looked like nobody had been down there in ages. Nice place, huh? I stepped on the first stair, and it creaked when I put my foot on it. I was scared to go down the rest of the steps because it seemed like they would break any minute, but I knew I had to. I kept walking down slowly, but after a stair almost broke under me, I decided that going faster would be better.

"Anyone else find this place creepy?" asked Roy.

"I do," I said.

When we got to the bottom of the stairs, we were in the dungeon. There weren't jail cells lined up on the sides like the fox had told me. In fact, it wasn't even a hall. It was a giant room that I couldn't even see the end of. On the walls, there were torches hung up, and Alex lit a few of them so we could see and he wouldn't have to keep a flame in his hand.

"Where's King Olkin supposed to be?" asked Xavier.

"I don't know, I thought there were going to be jail cells here," I responded.

"Well maybe you got wrong directions!" said Xavier.

"What can we do about it now?" I asked, "our only choice is to keep going."

I walked forward and my right foot sank about two inches into the ground. I looked down and I saw that the tile I had stepped on had sunk into the ground. I immediately heard a loud *snap!* but I couldn't tell what it was.

"Move!" shouted Lauren. I had learned to listen to her, so I quickly walked backwards a few steps. Suddenly, a giant two-sided ax swung down from the ceiling and nearly chopped my head off. The ax acted like a pendulum; swinging from side to side. It took up about three-fourths of the room at once, and would swing fairly fast; leaving less than a one second gap for someone to run through on either side.

"Oh no," I whispered to myself.

Chapter Twenty

"Well this complicates things," said Alex.

"We're not going to die," said Xavier sarcastically.

"Stay positive, that way, we have a better chance of surviving," I said.

"We'll have to go one at a time; really carefully," said Lauren, "each of us will get about two second to run through, so you'll have to time yourself perfectly."

"Great," said Alex, "who wants to go first?"

"I'll go," I said. I walked up to the ax and stood in front of it for a few seconds; deciding when to run. My heart started pounding so hard and fast in my ears, I could barely hear anything else. When the ax reached the left side of the room and was about to switch directions, I sprinted as fast as I could from the right wall. I could feel the wind of the ax on my back right after I ran through. I thought I was going to die, but I somehow made it, and so did everyone else.

"I can't believe that I made it here alive," said Roy.

"Well, we still haven't found King Olkin yet, look in front of you," said Xavier.

Xavier was right; we hadn't found him yet. The room hadn't turned into a hall, and there definitely weren't jail cells lined up on both sides, instead, there were platforms about two feet wide and two feet long. There were about three to four feet gaps between each platform and they were standing in place of the ground. It was even worse then the stairs.

"This could be a problem," I said.

"How are we going to survive this time?" asked Alex.

"It looks a lot like the cave we found Roy's orb in," I said, "maybe we can use the same technique."

"I'll go first this time," said Roy. The first platform was about one foot from where we were standing, so he went onto that one. Once he got on, the platform started tilting in all directions and Roy was stumbling while trying not to fall.

"Balance yourself!" shouted Lauren. Roy immediately put one foot on the front of the platform, and one on the back so it balanced him perfectly. I thought he would be alright until the platform started going down.

"What's happening?!" he shouted.

"Don't panic!" said Lauren, "Just do what I say!"

"Okay," he said nervously.

Chapter Twenty

"Slowly turn yourself around," said Lauren. Roy started turning himself by moving both feet in the same direction at the same time so the platform would stay balanced. By the time he was completely turned around, his head was about to go below ground level. His face looked completely panicked.

"Now just jump onto the ledge," said Lauren.

Roy bent his knees, and took a leap up and forward. He grabbed onto the ledge, and his right hand slipped off the gravel. He was barely hanging on with one hand, and there was no platform below him. Just by reflex, I bent down and tried to grab his hand. I got hold of his right hand with my left, and I pulled him up after grabbing his other arm, too.

I barely managed to pull him up, and after a little bit, he climbed up onto the stable ground again. I knew that getting to the other side would be trickier than I had originally thought. If you let yourself sink, there would be no way to get back up, and if you lost your balance, you would fall to your doom. I didn't exactly like our chances.

"So what's our plan this time?" asked Alex.

"The only way to do this is to go fast, and stay balanced," said Lauren.

"And how are we supposed to manage that?" asked Roy.

"Why doesn't Roy just make us some stairs so we can get to the bottom and walk across?" I asked hopefully.

"Let's just see what's down there first," said Lauren. She picked up a rock from the ground and dropped it off the ledge. I didn't hear anything for about thirty seconds, and that just told me how far down it was. I heard the rock splash, and then a bunch of echoed hissing.

"We now know that there is crocodile-infested water down there," said Lauren.

"Well that rules out my idea," I said.

"Maybe we could all hop across really fast," suggested Alex.

"That's too risky," said Lauren, "if you make the slightest wrong move, or lose your balance for even a second, you can fall and probably not survive."

"Then what can we do?" I asked.

Chapter Twenty

"Hey, did anyone else notice that the platform to the right of the one Roy stepped on was going up?" asked Xavier.

"No, but how does that help us?" I asked.

"If someone else goes on that platform, then they would both stay at ground level," he said.

"Then let's go," said Roy.

"Hold on," said Lauren, "if only two people can go at one time, then someone's got to either stay here, or hop across really quickly."

Right when he said that, I could hear rapid footsteps approaching us; apparently the foxes had found out that we were down there, "You guys go now, I'll figure something out!" I said.

"But—"

I cut Lauren off and said, "There's not much time before the foxes get here! You have to leave!" it seemed like the heroic thing to do at the time, but I soon realized it was a really stupid move on my part.

After they left, I had absolutely no way of getting across. I looked around, but all there was behind me was a giant ax swinging from a rope attached to the ceiling. I couldn't exactly tell where the ceiling was, but I knew that it was really high. Then I thought of a brilliant idea.

I could hear the footsteps getting louder and louder, which meant that they were getting closer and closer. I turned around and sliced the ax from the rope with some air. By that time, I could actually see some foxes behind the ax, but it fell on them soon after. I ran towards the rope and shot streams of air at the ground; making me shoot up. I grabbed onto the rope and started swinging back and forth.

I went as far forward as I could without hitting the ceiling, and I got too scared to jump. I was afraid that I would fall to my doom, but on the other hand, I didn't want to get devoured by an army of foxes. I went with the first option; I actually had a better chance of survival. I felt like I was Tarzan; swinging on a rope and I was just about to jump off to land somewhere far away. I let go of the rope at the point when I was closest to the other end, and I flew forwards. About ten seconds later, I landed on the complete other side of the platforms.

Surprisingly, I landed on my feet, but I fell to the ground seconds later because my knees couldn't handle the pressure. I had landed about one foot in front of Roy, and he stared at me with wide eyes, "Where did you come from?"

All four of them had just come onto the other side too, "I'll explain later. Right now, we have more important things to take care of; King Olkin is still here." I got up off my feet and took one step forward. My foot sank into the ground about one inch again, and I suddenly heard a rumbling noise coming from above us. I looked up, and I saw a giant, black, metal gate coming down about one hundred feet in front of us.

"Stop stepping on the dangerous tiles!" shouted Roy.

"Sorry," I said over the sound of the gate coming down.

"Run!" shouted Xavier at the top of his lungs. I sprinted as fast as I could, and I barely made it under the gate. The gate closed shut behind us with a loud *boom!* and I let out a breath I didn't know I was holding.

"I can't believe we're all still alive," said Xavier.

"I think we're finally here," I said. I looked on both sides of the hall, and there were finally jail cells lined up.

"So which cell is King Olkin in?" asked Alex.

We Meet the King

"The seventh one on the left side," I said; remembering the fox's directions. The jail cells were small cubes about six feet wide, four feet long and seven feet tall. There were sliding metal bars in front of each cell, just like in the wolves' castle. I walked up to the seventh one on the left side, and I saw a regular gray wolf curled up and sleeping in the corner.

"Is this him?" asked Roy.

"Only one way to find out," I said. I slid open the bars and the wolf woke up from the noise. It got up and bared its teeth at me. I put my hands up and said, "It's okay, we're friends." The wolf closed its mouth and just stood there.

"Are you King Olkin?" asked Alex.

"Yes," he responded.

"We're here to save you," I said.

"How do I know that I can trust you?" asked the wolf in his deep voice. I pulled out my sword and showed him the orb as proof that we had come to rescue him, "Okay, I'll believe you for now, but how are you planning to get me out of here?"

Chapter Twenty

"Just give us a minute and we'll figure it out," I said. I turned around and started talking to my friends.

"How are we supposed to get out of here?" asked Roy.

"I have no idea," I said.

"Hey wait," said Lauren, "Roy, you dug that trench really easily when we were fighting Bailey, right?"

"Yeah, I did," he responded.

"So maybe you can dig us a tunnel to get out," he suggested.

"Great idea," I said. I turned back to King Olkin and said, "Just follow us." He nodded.

We all moved away from the center of the cell, and Roy made a hole just big enough for someone to go through, "Everybody in," he said after dropping down into the hole.

Alex went next, and then Lauren, Xavier and King Olkin. I walked to the front of the cell and closed the bars. I then dropped into the hole and Roy closed it above me. The tunnel was really wide; about eight feet. Alex had a fire in her hands up front so we could all see. Every so often, Roy would close the tunnel behind us so that there was no evidence that we had left, and so nobody else would be able to come through.

"How far should we go?" asked Roy.

"As far away from this castle as we can get," I said. I noticed that King Olkin looked very weak compared to the other wolves I had seen. I didn't think that it was normal for him at least not from the story I had heard of how he became king, "Are you okay?" I asked him.

"I'm not sure," he said, "I think that the foxes were giving me some kind of poison, and I don't think I have much more time to live, so I must pass on a message to you before I die."

"Okay," I said. I didn't know if anyone else was listening, if they weren't, I would just tell them later.

"You know that there are two worlds that exist, correct?" asked King Olkin.

"Yeah, we came from the other world, why?" I said.

"Because, there are not only two, but three worlds," he said.

"What's the third world?" I asked.

"That is for you to find out. I have found a way to get there, and come back alive."

Chapter Twenty

"Why is this important right now?" I asked.

"Because, I am one of the only two that know this information. That is the real reason that the foxes captured me; they wanted information. They tried to force it out of me, but they never succeeded," King Olkin told me.

"So you're giving me the information?" I asked.

"Yes, but not entirely. You must go to the Temple of Souls, and prove that you are worthy. If it believes you, then you may pass. The only way to get to the Temple of Souls is with the code; otherwise you will never be able to find it. To find where I have hidden the code, you must solve this riddle: Beyond the Door of Fallen Riches lies a hidden fortune."

"Okay, I'll remember that," I said, "but who's the other person that knows this information?"

"He is one who will only use this information for himself. That is why I told you; you must save the world from him," said Olkin.

"But what's his name?" I asked.

"K-" King Olkin would have finished his sentence, but he fell over; not able to say anything. I guess he had been right; the foxes had been feeding him some poison, or something deadly.

"Guys!" I shouted.

"What?" asked Lauren. They all stopped walking and crowded around the fallen king.

"I-I think King Olkin either fainted or died," I said nervously.

Lauren put her hand on King Olkin's chest and she said, "There's no pulse."

"What can we do?" asked Alex.

"I think we should take him back to the wolves' kingdom so he can be properly buried; he deserves it," said Lauren.

"I'll carry him back," I said. I picked him up off the ground and he rested on my arms. He was incredibly heavy, so I knew that he was indeed dead. A few minutes later, Roy started making a staircase so we could get out of the tunnel. It was so dark in the cave that when I got outside, my eyes started burning.

We followed the map that Aric had drawn for us backwards to get to his house, and I knew the way back from there. We didn't stop at Aric's house for very long; I just told him what happened, but I didn't tell him what King Olkin had told me just before he passed away.

"So does that mean that your entire journey was pointless?" asked Aric.

"I guess so, but there was nothing we could do about it," I said.

We left soon after; Aric had given us some food and water, so we were all ready to go. The entire way back, nobody said a word; we were all thinking about something or the other. When we got to the front of the castle, I felt bad that probably one of the greatest kings that ever lived had died, and I was carrying him back. He had died while talking to me, so I felt even worse. I wondered how Kevdak would feel; one of his good friends was dead. We decided to tell him the news first.

We walked up to the front door and the wolves standing guard let us in. we walked into the king's room, but Kevdak wasn't there, so I asked one of the guards where he was. "He said he had some business in the dungeon to take care of," said the guard.

"Thanks," I responded. I still had King Olkin in my hands, so it was a bit harder to get in and out of doors, but it didn't matter much. Alex took us to the secret door that led to the dungeon, and we all went down the slope. When we got there, I looked to the end of the hall and I saw Kevdak talking to someone in a cell, and that had to be Bailey, seeing as he was the only one in a cell anymore.

"What do you think they're talking about?" whispered Roy.

"I don't know," I said, "do you want to find out?"

"Yes!" he whispered excitedly.

"How are we going to without them noticing we're here?" asked Alex.

"Hey, has anyone ever heard of directional sound?" asked Lauren.

"No, what's that?" I said.

"It's pretty self explanatory, it's basically a sound flashlight," she said.

"Interesting, but how does that help us?" I asked.

"Sound travels through air, right?" she said.

"Yeah, it does."

"So maybe you can make a small air tunnel that directs some of the sound just to us," suggested Lauren.

Chapter Twenty

"Sounds good," I said. I took a small bit of air from around where Kevdak and Bailey were talking and made a continuous stream of air that led directly to where we were standing. I could hear them talking softly, but that was all we wanted.

"I helped you become king, so you help me break out of here," said Bailey.

"Under one condition, you have to help me take over this world," said Kevdak.

"Why do you need my help?" asked Bailey.

"Because, you're the most powerful person in the world," said Kevdak.

"I was defeated by five boys, why don't you get their help to take over the world?" asked Bailey.

"They would never agree to this, they wouldn't understand the implications. They still care about King Olkin, and they might turn against me if I do one small thing wrong. You would never do that," said Kevdak.

"Fine, I'll help you, but you'll have to get my sword, and figure out a way to break down this stupid wall of stone."

We Meet the King

"Then you will help me take over this pitiful place," said Kevdak. I stopped the stream of air because I was in shock from what I had just heard.

I saw Kevdak finishing his conversation so I said to Roy, "Trench, now!" Roy made a trench and we all fell in. he closed it above us so Kevdak wouldn't know that we were there.

"You heard what I heard, right?" asked Roy.

"Yeah, there's only one explanation for what just happened," I said, "Kevdak's a traitor."

TO BE CONTINUED...

This page was intentionally left blank.

This page was intentionally left blank.

This page was intentionally left blank.

ABOUT THE AUTHOR

Ravi Pandya is an author, inventor with multiple patents under his name and a game developer. Ravi wrote this book when he was thirteen years old and in eighth grade. Ravi has many creative interests such as playing in symphonic and jazz bands; creating robots and has been a key member of California State champion team in robotics. He lives with his parents and sister in Northern California.